# MORE THAN COMICS

**Also by Elizabeth Briggs**

*More Than Exes*
*More Than Music*

# MORE THAN COMICS

## A CHASING THE DREAM NOVEL

# ELIZABETH BRIGGS

Cover Designed by Najla Qamber Designs
Model Photo by Mandy Hollis Photography
Models: Amee Thompson and Julio Elving

ISBN (paperback) 1507859376
ISBN-13 978-1507859377
ISBN (ebook) 978-0-9915696-2-5

www.elizabethbriggs.net

For Gary
My Comic-Con partner in crime

# CHAPTER ONE
## TARA

A trio of Ghostbusters bumped my shoulder, knocking me into a group of Disney princesses. I muttered a quick apology and continued through the mob, ignoring people at booths handing out flyers, swag bags, and free comics. I could barely breathe with so many bodies packed tight around me, at least half of which were in costume.

Welcome to San Diego Comic-Con, aka nerd paradise. Four days of shameless geekiness and a celebration of every fandom you could possibly think of. If you could watch it, read it, or play it, someone was probably cosplaying as a character from it.

I was in heaven.

Or at least I would be in heaven if not for the butterflies in my stomach.

Ugh. Butterflies in my stomach, seriously? Talk about a cliché. As a writer I shouldn't even be *thinking* in clichés. But I was about to speak on a panel about my graphic novel, followed by my first ever book signing. At Comic-Con, of all places. It was both my dream come true and an introvert's worst nightmare. Nothing had prepared me for the sheer enormity of the four-day event, or the chaos created by hundreds of thousands of people packed into the convention center. I couldn't decide whether I wanted to jump up and down and cheer, or curl up in a dark corner and rock back and forth until it was all over.

But, if I was honest with myself, the real reason for those damn butterflies was the fact that I was about to meet Hector, the artist of my graphic novel, in person for the first time.

I wasn't sure *why* I was so nervous about meeting him, either. I shouldn't be nervous. We'd been friends for years, after all. But…what if it was weird when we met face to face, without computer screens and thousands of miles between us? What if we didn't know what to say or how to act around each other? What if the connection we had online didn't translate into real life?

What if we just didn't click offline?

I forced my way through the crowd toward the Black Hat Comics booth. As the third largest comic book publisher, after

Marvel and DC, they had a huge booth right in the middle of the exhibit hall. It could be spotted from anywhere inside thanks to the giant black wizard hat stretching all the way to the ceiling, covered in hundreds of little twinkling stars.

There was no sign of Hector yet, but I spotted the trim, dark goatee and wire-frame glasses of our editor Miguel, who stood behind a table with free post cards, buttons, magnets, and sample comics.

"Hey, Tara," he said, giving me a quick hug. "Good to see you again. Are you ready for your panel?"

"I hope so."

"I know you'll do great. We're just waiting for Hector now and then we'll head up to the room."

I shuffled out of the way of someone carrying a huge box of action figures into the booth. I stepped back and the crowd swallowed me up, blocking my view, and I had to fight my way through.

When I emerged, Hector stood beside Miguel, shaking hands and making their introductions. His mouth curled into a slight grin as our eyes made contact. My heart skipped a beat at the sight—another cliché, but given the circumstances, could anyone blame me?

He was so much *bigger* in person than I'd imagined. Not just tall, but broad and muscular, too. I'd seen him through a webcam, in photos, and on *The Sound*, but I had never seen the full package up close like this.

Nothing had prepared me for how large and masculine he'd be in real life.

Or how insanely hot he would be.

He'd always been good looking, of course. But in person he was mouth-wateringly gorgeous, the living embodiment of tall, dark, and handsome, with curly hair peeking out from under his Villain Complex baseball cap, smooth, bronze skin, and warm, brown eyes I could fall into forever.

And his arms! His arms deserved sonnets written about them. They were huge—probably as big as my thighs, and all muscle. I had the strongest urge to wrap my hands around them and see if they were as hard as they looked. For a brief moment I imagined him sliding those arms around me and lifting me up, and how good they would feel as they brought me to his lips...

Hold on, where had that image come from? I'd never thought about Hector in that way before. We'd always just been friends. That was it.

"Great, you're both here," Miguel said, bringing me out of my trance. "I have to talk to someone for a minute, and then I'll take you both to your panel, okay?"

He disappeared into the booth and I stared up at Hector, unable to speak. I didn't know how to react now that we were together. Should I hug him? Shake his hand? Kiss him on the cheek? I had no idea what the correct social protocol was when you met an online friend in person for the first time.

"Hector..." His name was the only thing I could manage to

say. Words, usually my closest friends, seemed to have abandoned me completely. Maybe it was those arms that were making me crazy. I'd always had a thing for guys' arms. Not to mention those broad shoulders and that toned chest, wow. His black t-shirt did nothing to hide the contours of his abs, and all I could think about was what he would look like without that thin fabric in the way.

Okay, those thoughts? They had to stop. This was just a silly rush of emotions from finally meeting him in person after so many years. Nothing more.

"Hey, Tara." He'd been checking me out, too. It was like we both needed to drink in the sight of each other before we could process that this was real life and not a dream.

I gave up on trying to figure out the correct social protocol and threw myself against him, into that hard chest and those incredible biceps. He wasn't really a hugger, from what he'd told me anyway, but I couldn't stop myself. I was just so happy that we were really together, face to face, after so long.

He didn't seem to mind. His arms circled my back and he pulled me tight against him, his face pressing into my hair. I heard his heart pounding as he held me and he smelled so good, like pine or something equally masculine. I could have stayed like that for hours, but I pulled back before it could get awkward.

"It's so good to meet you in person," I managed to get out.

His hands lingered on my arms, like he didn't want to let go of me either. "Finally."

"I know, I can't believe it took us three years." I studied his face, so different in three dimensions, yet nearly as familiar as my own reflection. Something about him looked off, like he didn't quite line up with my mental image of him, but I couldn't tell what. "It almost doesn't feel real. It's like I know you so well, but at the same time, I don't know you at all."

"It *is* strange. But you do know me. Better than almost anyone."

He looked so serious when he said that, so intense, that I wasn't sure how to respond. Instead I hugged him again. This time he didn't return it quite as hard.

"Sorry," I said, pulling away from him. "I know you don't like hugs."

"I'll make an exception for you." He had yet to take his eyes off me, even in the middle of all the chaos around us, and it made me feel warm all over. I couldn't stop smiling.

"Where's the rest of the band?"

"They're around somewhere." He finally looked away as he said it, like he was scanning the crowd for them.

"I can't wait to meet them. I feel like I know them already, after hearing so much about them over the years and watching you all on *The Sound*."

"That reminds me." He fished around in his pocket, and then shoved something into my hand. "Here."

"What's this?"

"A ticket and backstage pass for our show tonight. If you

want to come, that is. You don't have to." He pulled off his Villain Complex baseball cap and ran his fingers through his hair. "You probably already have plans, huh? With Andy?"

"No, no plans." I played with the edge of the ticket, my stomach clenching at the thought of Andy. "I'd love to see you perform in person. I'll be there."

"Cool." He shoved his baseball cap back on, and I realized what was different about him.

"You cut your hair!" It was much shorter, trimmed close to his head now, though a hint of his glorious dark curls remained on top. It was a good look on him. A little more mature. I wished he'd take his hat off again.

He shrugged. "It was getting really long. Thought I'd get it cut before the tour."

"I like it. Although I loved your hair when it was long, too."

"You did?" Surprise flickered across his face. After years of video chatting I knew his expressions well.

"Of course. You have gorgeous hair." Oops, I'd probably said too much, but oh well. It was the truth.

Miguel returned and clasped us each on the arm. "All ready for your panel? Let's head on up."

I reluctantly tore my gaze from Hector and smiled at Miguel. "Ready."

Miguel led us out the exhibit hall and up an escalator to the second floor of the convention center. He gave us a quick rundown of our schedule for the next four days and I nodded and asked him a few questions. Hector didn't say anything, but he wasn't much of a small talker. He was the kind of guy who didn't waste words or speak just to fill silence, and when he did speak up it was honest and direct. I'd always liked that about him.

"This way," Miguel said, leading us past different meeting rooms with long lines outside them, composed of hundreds of people sitting along the walls and chatting with each other, playing on their phones, or reading comics. Hector and I walked close behind him through a surging crowd that moved like a herd of sheep, mindlessly pushing forward in either direction. It was all we could do not to get lost in it, and I clutched my Comic-Con badge tightly, worried it would fall off in the commotion.

A group of Assassin's Creed cosplayers stopped to pose for a photo and Hector had to dodge them. He bumped against my side, making me jump. "Nervous?" he asked.

"A little." I forced myself to let go of my badge. "I've never done a panel or anything like this before. I'm worried I'll say something stupid or just freeze up entirely."

"Nah. Won't happen. You'll do great."

We were forced to stop and wait while the Comic-Con volunteers ushered a massive line into Ballroom 20, blocking our path. "Are you nervous?" I asked, as the stream of people rushed past us.

He gave a little shrug. "Not really."

"No, you never seem to get nervous. Not even when you're on stage in front of hundreds of people, or on TV for the entire country to see."

"I get nervous. Just not on stage. Maybe if I was up front I'd get nervous, but when I'm in the back, behind my drums, I just…zone out. My hands know what to do and as long as I shut my mind off I'm fine. Same with this kind of stuff. The less I worry about it the better. That might work for you, too."

"Maybe." The volunteers capped off the line and let us pass, and we chased after Miguel down the long hall. "So when *do* you get nervous?"

Hector glanced over at me. His mouth opened, but then he looked away and scowled.

"Oh no," I said, punching him lightly on the arm. "Now you have to tell me."

His eyes dropped to the spot I'd touched him, still frowning. "I was nervous today, but not because of the panel." He raised those dark eyes to meet mine again. "Because I was meeting you."

"Really?" Hearing that made me feel a lot better. All those butterflies in my stomach vanished. "I was nervous, too."

"Yeah?"

I laughed. "Well, you *are* a famous rock star now."

"Not true. And you knew me long before all that."

I nudged him with my shoulder. "Then I guess neither of us had anything to be nervous about."

He gave me a rare smile, making him even more handsome. "No. I guess not."

# CHAPTER TWO
## HECTOR

Tara kept touching me. Normally I didn't like people touching me, but when she did it I wanted more. Only problem was it made it hard to focus on anything but her.

She was even hotter in person, in dark jeans and a tight *Firefly* t-shirt that showed off her large breasts, curvy hips, and delicious ass. Soft and feminine, yet without being so small I thought I'd crush her. With a body like that it was hard not to stare, but the rest of her was fucking amazing, too.

Her long, golden hair fell around her shoulders and I wanted to see if it felt as silky as it looked. But the thing that rendered me completely helpless was the way her blue eyes lit up when she smiled. No, not just blue, but sapphire. Cobalt. The color I'd use to paint a dark sky.

And the sound of her laugh—damn, I wanted to do whatever I could to hear it again. It was a reminder that she was warm and friendly and everything I was not. I was a dark cloud and she was the ray of sunshine that somehow managed to break through.

Maybe that's why I'd been in love with her for as long as I could remember.

"Here's the room," Miguel said, stopping in front of an open door with a long line next to it. A quick glance inside showed that the room was completely packed, too. It wasn't a huge one, especially compared to some of the others we'd passed, but there were a few hundred people inside at least.

"Are all those people here for us?" I asked.

"Yep. Great turnout, huh? I asked them to switch us to a larger room, but they couldn't do it."

"Oh shit." I knew our graphic novel had been doing pretty well, especially after my band was on *The Sound*, but I had no idea so many people would come to hear us talk about it. I thought we'd get maybe ten people, tops.

I hadn't been lying to Tara—I wasn't nervous before, but now that I saw the massive crowd I realized I wasn't prepared for any of this. Fuck, what if people asked me questions?

I should have asked Jared for advice or something. As lead singer for our band, he'd handled all the interviews and publicity stuff when we'd been on *The Sound*. At first it had pissed me off when he'd completely hogged the camera and made it seem like the band was all about him, but eventually I'd realized it was better that way. He was good at that shit and the rest of us hated it. And it's not like I wanted to be in the spotlight either. That's why I was a drummer and not a guitarist. Well, that and because beating the shit out of drums was way more fun.

"Wow, this is so overwhelming," Tara said. Her gaze swept across the crowd of people waiting for us, taking it all in—but I only had eyes for her. She turned to me, catching me staring, but I couldn't look away. I was held hostage by her flushed cheeks and kissable lips.

I'd memorized her face and heard her voice a thousand times, but seeing her up close, in real life, was different. All those feelings I'd tried to bury came rushing back to the surface and made it hard for me to breathe. I'd hoped meeting her would make me get over my stupid crush, but instead it had only gotten worse. The real Tara was so much better than even my best fantasy of her.

Christie, the moderator for our panel, arrived and introduced herself to us. She ran a comics site focused on diversity and was about the same age as Tara and me, with long black hair streaked with pink and a little stud in her nose.

We shook hands and she grinned at us. "I'm so excited for this panel. I begged them to let me moderate it cause I'm a huge fan of *Misfit Squad*. I'm dying for the next one to come out!"

"I remember the feature you did on it," Tara said. "We're so grateful for your support."

We walked into the room together and the crowd hushed. Christie, Tara, and I each took a seat at a table on a raised platform in front of a wall plastered with the Comic-Con logo. Name placards were placed in front of us, each of which had something on the back about watching our language because there were members of the audience under eighteen.

"They're talking to you here," Tara said, pointing at the warning.

I gave her my best innocent look. "Hey, I can be good."

"Uh huh." She scanned the room again, taking it all in with wide eyes. "I still can't believe we're on a panel at Comic-Con. This has been my dream forever and now it's real. It's all happening!"

Damn, she was so beautiful it was almost hard to look at her. I loved seeing her this happy and watching all her hard work pay off. "*You* made this happen."

Her smile got even bigger, bathing me in its glow. "We made it happen together."

"Nah, all I did was draw a few things."

"Oh, stop being so modest," she said, swatting at my arm. More touching. Yes, please.

I wasn't good with words—I left that to her and to Jared—but I had the strongest urge to pull out my sketchbook and draw the way she'd looked when we'd first seen each other in person, to capture her eyes meeting mine and her face brightening when she recognized me. I never wanted to forget the way she'd looked in that moment. For a brief second I'd thought it possible she could love me back.

And then it was over.

She'd never once hinted that she wanted to be more than friends, and I knew she never would—she'd been dating Andy for the past year and she was about to start a job in New York. Meeting in person wouldn't change anything between us.

Which is why she could never know how I felt about her.

Miguel propped up the first book of *Misfit Squad* on the table between us, gave us a thumbs up, and disappeared into the back of the room.

"Welcome to the *Misfit Squad* panel," our moderator said, into her mic. "I'm Christie Yamamoto from the *Diversity In Comics* website. This is one of my favorite graphic novels ever, and I'm so happy to be here with the writer, Tara McFadden, and the artist, Hector Fernandez."

The audience applauded and all the hundreds of faces blurred together, like when I was on stage at a show—except for four familiar ones in the back of the crowd. Jared sat there in a t-shirt with a bunch of classic villains on it like Dracula, Frankenstein, and The Wolfman. His arm was around his girlfriend Maddie, who was also our guitarist. Next to them was his brother Kyle, our keyboardist, along with his girlfriend, Alexis.

I shook my head at them, but a grin slipped through. I'd told them not to come to the panel because if I messed up royally I didn't want them to see it, but their smiling faces actually made me feel calmer. I'd never admit it out loud, but I was secretly glad they'd ignored me.

Christie held up a copy of the first book and the room quieted down. "*Misfit Squad* is out now and if you haven't read it yet, it's about a teenage girl whose power is breaking things. When she's rejected by her city's superhero group, she and some others with equally undesirable or 'useless' powers form their own group instead. Together they have to learn to control their powers and resist turning into the villains people *think* they are, while saving the city from the so-called superheroes, who turn out to be the real villains."

She launched into our bios next, explaining how Tara had worked on different comics at Black Hat before writing *Misfit Squad*. It was pretty impressive that she'd done so much already, considering she'd just graduated with her English degree a month ago.

Next Christie described how I'd also worked on various comics while in art school and mentioned I was the drummer for Villain Complex, which had come in second on the reality TV show *The Sound* a week earlier. That got lots of cheers and I ducked my head a little, wishing I hadn't worn my Villain Complex hat. I hoped people in the audience were actually fans of *Misfit Squad* and not just the band, especially for Tara's sake.

"Tara, let's start with you," Christie said. "Where did you get the idea for *Misfit Squad*?"

Tara gave me a wide-eyed look, but leaned into the mic and started speaking. "I always loved comics, but had a hard time relating to them because the heroes in them were so much cooler than me." That got a little laugh from the audience. "One day I joked to a friend that if I was a superhero my power would be something no one would want, like breaking things. Then I started thinking about how that could actually be a pretty cool power, if you could learn to control it...and began coming up with other powers that at first seemed stupid or useless, but weren't. I pitched it to the guys at Black Hat and they loved the idea, and that's how *Misfit Squad* all began."

"Very cool," Christie said. "I think one reason *Misfit Squad* has such a huge following already is because it's a true underdog story. So many people relate to your characters and how they're outcasts, both among normal people and other superheroes, until they find each other and start their own group and become almost a family. Was that something you wanted to write about specifically?"

Tara relaxed a little, smiling at Christie. "That's definitely one thing I wanted to emphasize because I think if you're a little weird growing up, or something of an outcast, like I imagine all of us here are...." That got another chuckle from the audience. "Then you never *really* feel comfortable around most people. Especially your family, who probably never seemed to understand you. But as you grow up you find others like yourself, people who support you, embrace your weirdness, and love you for who you are—and they become your new family." She looked at me with this last line, and my heart constricted in my chest. She was killing me here.

"Comic-Con is definitely one big, crazy family," Christie said, with a laugh. "Hector, how did you become involved in the project?"

Shit, that question was for me. I focused on my band's faces in the audience—my own second family—and tried to relax. "After Tara wrote the script for the first book she put out feelers all over the Internet, in artist forums and places like that, looking for someone who might be interested in working on it. She had a random page's script...I think it was page 33 or something?"

I looked at her to confirm, and she laughed. "I don't think that page even exists in the final version. It got cut."

"Oh yeah, I forgot about that. Anyway, it was a good way in, with some fun action and dialogue. I loved the premise and the characters immediately from that short bit of script and knew I had to draw it. I put together a full page panel and submitted it." I shrugged. "I guess she liked it, because she chose me."

"There were a lot of good entries, but I knew Hector was the one the moment I saw his art. It was just so perfect for what I had in mind."

"The artwork is truly remarkable," Christie said. "It really brings the story to life. But tell me about your working relationship. I heard the two of you had never met in person until now. Is that true?"

"That's true," Tara said. "I live in Boston and Hector lives in Los Angeles, so we did all our work together online, through video chats and email, stuff like that. But we talk just about every day, so I feel like we've been friends forever."

"What was it like working with each other?"

"Tara's great to work with," I said. "She has a strong vision for her series but is also open to any suggestions I have."

"And Hector has some brilliant ideas, too. The books all changed a lot—for the better—thanks to his input. They became a true collaboration between the two of us. They're not just my books, but *our* books."

Tara gave me that brilliant smile again and I wanted to kiss her so bad. It meant a lot to me that she thought that about *Misfit Squad*'cause I loved those books almost as much as I loved her. I'd put a lot of blood, sweat, and tears into them, and it was easily my best work. I was proud of what we'd created together.

"Another thing I love about *Misfit Squad* is how diverse it is," Christie continued. "There are characters of all different races, queer characters, even overweight and disabled characters. You don't see those too often in comics."

"That was really important to both of us." Tara glanced at me and I nodded. "We wanted to tell a story that had characters who weren't typical superheroes, and that included some who weren't white or straight or didn't have ideal bodies."

I leaned in to the mic and added, "And we wanted to make sure lots of different people could read the book and see themselves in it. That's something I never had when I was growing up and reading comics as a Mexican kid."

"Great point," Christie said.

Over the next few minutes she continued to ask us about the books and what was next for the series, before opening the panel to questions from the audience. In the middle of the room dozens of people scrambled to get in line in front of a microphone. Who knew so many people would have questions for us?

One of the Comic-Con volunteers waved a guy in a Green Lantern t-shirt to the mic. "Hey," he said. "Big fan of both *Misfit Squad* and Villain Complex. My question is for Hector. How do you balance being both a successful comic book artist and a drummer in a popular band? Is there one you consider your focus and the other your hobby, or are they both equal to you?"

"Good question," Tara said, turning to me. "I'm curious about this, too."

Damn, these people didn't mess around. They couldn't have started me off with an easy one?

His question was something I'd started to worry about with the band going on tour this month and preparing to record our second album soon. Tara and I hadn't discussed it, but with her starting a new job too it was something we'd have to address at some point if we wanted to do more than three books.

"They're equally important to me. I don't consider myself a drummer first and an artist second, or vice versa. I'm both all the time. Sometimes it's tough to find time to do both, and maybe it'll be even harder now, but I'll always find a way to make them each a priority. If you love doing something, if you feel drawn to it above everything else, nothing can stop you from pursuing it. I'm just weird because I feel that way about two things." I rubbed the back of my neck. I hadn't meant to talk so much, and worried I'd sounded stupid or boring. "I hope that answers your question."

"Thank you," the guy said, and was replaced at the mic by a girl in a Villain Complex shirt.

"Hi Hector! I just wanted to know, what is Jared like in person? And is he here, by any chance?"

In the back of the room, Jared sank lower in his chair and covered his mouth, trying not to laugh. Of course he would love that question, damn egomaniac. I wanted to roll my eyes but I kept my expression as neutral as I could while I answered. "Jared is a great guy and a very talented musician. Next question."

The girl looked disappointed but the Comic-Con volunteer shuffled her off and brought up the next girl, this one in a *Sailor Moon* costume.

"So now that Jared's taken, you're the only single guy in the band, right?" She batted her eyelashes at me suggestively, and a few people in the audience hooted.

I stared at her for a beat. "Is that really your question?"

She giggled. "Well, if you *are* single, do you want to go out later?"

I had no response to this. I wasn't used to being hit on like Jared or Kyle. My eyes found my friends again, who all looked like they were trying not to die of laughter. Yeah, laugh it up, assholes.

Tara patted me on the arm while smiling at the audience, as though she was amused by the question. "He's single and he's quite a catch, but I suspect you'll have to fight off a lot of girls for him."

I stared at her, wishing she hadn't said that. I didn't want to be single. I didn't want girls fighting over me. I wanted to be *hers*.

Sailor Moon was replaced by a girl in a tight, colorful dress. I couldn't tell if it was a costume or just how she dressed. "My question is um…what was it *really* like being on *The Sound*?"

Give me a fucking break.

I leaned forward, close to the mic. "Okay, I'm going to answer one more question about my band and that's it, so listen up. Being on *The Sound* was an amazing experience and did great things for our band, but it was also the craziest and most stressful and exhausting month of my entire life. It's awesome that so many of you are fans of the band, but this panel isn't about that. We're here to talk about *Misfit Squad*, so no more questions about the band or the show or my fucking personal life. You can come to our signing and ask me whatever you want there. But right now, someone needs to ask Tara a question."

So much for not swearing. I sat back and crossed my arms, and Tara gave me a reassuring smile. A huge chunk of the line left and went back to their seats, which made me even more annoyed. I hated that they'd made this about me and not about her, or what we'd created together.

"Yes, please keep your questions focused on the book," Christie said. She turned to the two of us, with a teasing smile. "Though I think we're all wondering—*is* there something going on between you two?"

Oh, shit.

# CHAPTER THREE
## TARA

"**S**orry about that," Hector said when the panel was over and we were leaving the room to head to our signing. "I didn't realize they'd just want to ask about the show and all that."

Oh, thank god. I thought he was apologizing for that *other* question. But if he was ignoring it, then so was I. Especially after he'd so quickly denied that we were anything more than friends.

Which was true, of course.

"It's okay," I said. "I don't mind. Your success with the band sold lots of copies of our book, so I can't complain."

"Yeah, but I don't want people to see *Misfit Squad* as 'that graphic novel by the drummer in the band on *The Sound*.' I want them to see it as this kick-ass book you wrote and I happened to do the art for."

"Why can't it be both? If your band's popularity introduced more people to our book, then that's great. Really, I don't mind. I think it's good for us. It might mean we can do a fourth book, thanks to you."

He stopped in the middle of the busy hallway and turned to face me, his expression serious. "I just don't want to steal your spotlight. When Jared and I were on *The Sound*, the show made it all about him and it drove me crazy. I don't ever want to take this away from you."

I placed my hand on his forearm and smiled up at him. "You're not. I promise."

His body relaxed and he nodded. I wasn't sure why he was so worried about this, but it touched me that he cared so much. That he wanted this to be special for me. He had no idea that just meeting him in person had already made it special.

We caught up with Miguel and he led us through a giant, bright room packed with people in costumes rushing around or taking photos of each other. Our signing table was against one wall and there was already an enormous line beside it. I should have expected it, with the huge turnout for the panel, but I was still blown away seeing so many people waiting for us. There had to be hundreds of them there, all waiting for our signatures.

One end of the table had boxes with copies of *Misfit Squad* in it, ready to be sold to people in line. I'd brought special pens for our signing, pretty metallic ones in different colors, but Miguel also provided some boring, black Sharpies. As we sat, Hector picked one up and twirled it, like I'd seen him do with his drumsticks. He didn't even look at the pen, as if he didn't realize he was doing it. Under the table his left leg bounced, very close to my own. I had the sudden urge to put my hand on his thigh, to see if it would relax him. Or to see if it felt as muscular as it looked. Luckily the first people in line rushed forward before I could do it.

A girl in a Captain Marvel shirt shoved a well-read copy of *Misfit Squad* at me with a smile. I opened it to the title page. My first signed book. How mind-blowing was that? It still shocked me to see the book in person, this thing that Hector and I had spent three years working on together. It was even more incredible seeing actual proof that strangers were reading it and not just my friends.

"I love this book so much," the girl said. "When's the next one coming out?"

"Thanks! The second one's out in September." I finished signing my name, with a signature I'd practiced for a week to make sure it looked cool and was different from the one I used on checks and stuff. I pushed the book over to Hector and his arm brushed against mine as he signed. I watched his wrist flex as the pen moved, momentarily stunned by how he could make something so basic look so sexy.

He was left handed. How had I never known that before?

The line continued forward, until a guy with black-rimmed glasses and blond hair poking out of a beanie slid a book in front of me, along with a business card. "Hi Tara. I work for Giselle Roberts, the producer. She'd like to set up a meeting with you during Comic-Con, if you have time."

I blinked at him, wondering if I'd heard him correctly. Giselle Roberts was the biggest female producer and showrunner around. She was known for bringing diverse TV shows to the major networks and then dominating the ratings with them. She'd also created many popular reality TV shows like *Behind The Seams, American Supermodel,* and *Road Trip Race.*

"I'd love to," I said. "Do you know why?"

He pulled out his phone, checking something on it. "She didn't tell me, but I know she's a fan. Can you sign the book to her? And are you free tomorrow at all?"

"Sure." I raised an eyebrow at Hector, who shrugged. We both signed the book while the guy set up a meeting before walking away, leaving me completely baffled.

"What was that about?" Hector asked.

"Your guess is as good as mine."

"Hmm. Maybe she wants to turn *Misfit Squad* into a TV show?"

"No, then she'd want to meet with you, too." I couldn't figure it out, but the line moved at a brisk pace and I didn't have any more time to ponder it.

For the next hour we signed so many books my wrist began

to throb. By the end of it I could barely move my hand and we'd run out of books to sell, although many fans had brought their own copies, too. And though some people were there because they'd seen Hector on *The Sound*, others seemed to genuinely love the book and were excited for the next one.

When it was over we said goodbye to Miguel and headed for the lobby of the convention center. "That was crazy," Hector said, running a hand through his short curls before covering them with his hat again. "I never expected so many people to show up."

"Me either. It was such a rush." I flexed my wrist. "Except now my hand hurts."

"It does? Mine seems okay."

"You're always using your hands, what with drawing and playing the drums. This was probably nothing to you."

He offered me his hand. "Let me help."

I rested my palm flat against his and little tingles shot through me. We were so close to holding hands. Touching like this was still in the realm of friendship, but at the same time, so incredibly intimate.

"Your hands are so tiny," he said, examining them.

"Or yours are just really big," I teased.

It was true, his were much larger than mine and his long, rough fingers completely dominated my own. What did they say about guys with big hands? Or was that feet? A quick glance down showed that those were big, too. I had to forcibly stop myself from checking the front of his jeans next.

He began to massage my wrist and his touch was firm but gentle. It was all I could do not to melt into a puddle right there. Time seemed to slip away, the crowd around us vanished, and I never wanted him to stop what he was doing.

"How's that?" he asked, releasing my hand and jolting me out of my trance.

I flexed my wrist and the pain was gone. His fingers were magic. I briefly wondered what else they could do. God, I needed to get my mind out of the gutter. "Much better. Thank you."

He nodded and glanced around the lobby, but didn't take another step. This was where we were supposed to split up and go our separate ways, but I got the feeling we were both stalling. I didn't want to say goodbye to him just yet either.

"Do you want to get coffee or something?" I asked. "A late lunch?"

He gave me another of his elusive smiles. "I'd like that."

We exited the convention center and joined the sea of people outside. The Gaslamp Quarter of downtown San Diego was almost as packed as inside the exhibit hall, with people hanging out in front of bars and restaurants, walking down the sidewalk to get to their hotels or one of the many off-site events, or standing around handing out flyers or trying to sell water bottles. The sun beat down on us, and I wasn't envious of anyone in costume in this heat.

We didn't talk much as we walked through the crowded streets other than to point out some of the things we saw, like cops pretending to make arrests for charity so people could take photos to send to friends or post online. Or the hundreds of ads and billboards for movies, TV shows, and video games that covered everything from the sides of buildings to the pedicabs and taxis in the street. Or the restaurants that had been completely taken over and transformed for the week, such as a café that had been redone for an upcoming zombie TV show, complete with undead servers and food made to look like brains and other mangled body parts. The menu alone made me want to gag. Needless to say, we decided not to eat there.

Every time I glanced at Hector, he met my gaze and his lips twitched into a small grin. Nope, we'd definitely had nothing to be nervous about. Being with him in person, even if we weren't saying a word, was just as easy as being with him online.

"How about here?" he asked, stopping outside a restaurant that looked fairly empty, possibly because it hadn't bothered with a fun theme. "Thai food is your favorite, right?"

"It is. How did you know?"

"You always eat it when we're on deadline and all stressed out, so I figured…." He shrugged.

"Huh. I never realized that, but you're right. It *is* my go-to comfort food." I tilted my head, smiling at him. "I'm impressed. But hey, *I* know you're allergic to seafood and you hate bananas and coconut. Oh, and your favorite food is your grandmother's tres leches cake."

His eyebrows shot up. "That's true. But I know *you're* addicted to Diet Coke."

"That's an easy one. Everyone knows that."

"Okay, how about this: you love chocolate but hate chocolate-flavored things. Chocolate cake, ice cream, milkshakes—all of those are out. The one exception is hot chocolate. Oh, and brownies. Can't forget those either."

I couldn't help but laugh. "Fine, I admit that you know me pretty well, too."

"Damn straight I do."

We got a table and ordered some food to share—he let me pick, since it was my favorite—and then launched right into easy conversation. He told me all about being on *The Sound*, since we hadn't been able to talk much while he was on it. It had only ended a week ago, and now he gave me all the behind-the-scenes scoop—how the producers had manipulated the results so Villain Complex couldn't win, how Jared and Maddie had carried on a secret relationship that nearly broke up the band, and how even though they hadn't won the show they'd gotten offers from multiple record labels for their second album.

"Dan is handling the negotiations now," he said, referring to the band's manager, who had been their mentor on *The Sound*. "But we've basically locked in a two-album deal with one of the labels. We plan to start working on new songs as soon as we get back from the tour."

"Wow, that's wonderful. It happened so fast!" I took a sip of my Diet Coke. "I'm *dying* to see you perform live. I watched the show on TV, of course, but it's not the same."

He picked up a chopstick and twirled it like one of his drumsticks. "So you're coming tonight?"

"Definitely."

"You probably need another ticket, huh? For Andy?"

I played with my napkin, avoiding Hector's gaze. "No, just one. I'm flying solo for a change."

"No? I thought you'd be here with him."

"He's at Comic-Con somewhere, I think, but not with me..." I'd been hoping to avoid talking about Andy. Or thinking about Andy. The wound was still so raw. But Hector deserved to know the truth. "We broke up a few days ago."

The chopstick hit the table with a soft clatter. "I'm sorry."

"Thanks." I sucked in a breath, trying to keep my voice steady. "It was a mutual thing. We both figured it was time to end it now that we've graduated. He's moving to Dallas and I'm moving to New York, so it's for the best, really."

Hector was silent for a moment, and I couldn't read his expression. "You were together for a year. That must be rough."

"Yeah." I sighed. "It's weird not talking to him anymore. I know we both have to move on with our lives, but it's hard saying goodbye to someone who was such an important part of mine for the last year."

I dropped my gaze to the table, wishing I hadn't said so

much. I'd always been pretty open with Hector about my personal life, but now it felt wrong, like I shouldn't be discussing my ex with him. "Anyway, it's over and I'm ready to move on. What about you? You *are* single, right? Or did I mislead your fans at the panel?"

"No, I'm not seeing anyone."

Of course not. Hector had been single for the entire time I'd known him. I wasn't sure why, but I knew it had something to do with his past. If he hadn't told me by now then I figured it wasn't any of my business. Still, I couldn't help but wonder…

The food arrived, steaming plates of pad thai and prik king. We changed the subject back to work, to discuss ideas for a fourth *Misfit Squad* book. Miguel wanted a proposal with the first few pages and an outline for the rest, which I'd already written up and sent to Hector so he could start on the artwork.

"I put a few rough sketches together," he said. "If you like them, I'll get to work on them ASAP."

"Do you have time? You're on tour for the next month…"

"I'll make time."

He pulled his sketchbook from where he always kept it—tucked under his shirt in the back of his jeans—and flipped it open. He angled the page toward me, careful not to get it too close to the food.

"Wow, this is perfect." I slid the sketchbook closer to me. Hector always brought my scripts to life in ways I never expected, that were even better than I had imagined. He took my ideas, my story, and infused himself into them with his artwork, so the final version was truly a collaboration between us. Each book of *Misfit Squad* had both of our souls in it.

A waiter carrying a tray of food bumped my elbow and I dropped the sketchbook on the floor. Hector and I both reached for it but I managed to grab it first. Except now it was open to a different page.

This one had a drawing of a beautiful girl. It was in black and white and more realistic than his comic book art, and you could see the care Hector had taken with it. The girl was smiling, her head slightly tilted, her long blond hair (or I assumed it was blond, from the shading) flowing around her shoulders. Pieces like this reminded me just how remarkable of an artist Hector was. How he could capture someone so perfectly with just a charcoal pencil and infuse so much emotion and beauty into a simple drawing.

And then I realized the girl was *me*.

Hector reached across the table and snatched the sketchbook out of my hands. My eyes jumped to his face, and he looked pained. Like someone had just punched him in the gut. Was he worried I wouldn't like it? How could he possibly think that?

"Hector, that…that was stunning."

"It's nothing," he said, shoving the sketchbook back in his jeans.

"I didn't know…" I stopped, taking a breath. "I mean, I never realized you'd drawn me before."

He shrugged and took a long chug of his water. "I draw everyone," he finally said.

Maybe that was true, but I *knew* Hector's artwork. I'd seen hundreds of his drawings, both art for *Misfit Squad* and random sketches he did for fun. There had been something different about that picture of me. Something special. Something more…intimate.

"Hector, do you…" I faltered, trying to come up with a better way to ask the questions threatening to burst out of me. "Is this…" No, that wasn't right. I tried a new approach. "Why didn't you ever show me?"

He still wouldn't look at me. "It's not a big deal."

That didn't answer the question at all. My fingers tightened around the chain at my neck, the metal biting into my skin a welcome distraction from how uncomfortable this moment was. "Are there others of me in there? Can I see?"

"No!"

His harsh response made me jump. I banged my knee against the table, causing the silverware and plates to rattle, and he cringed at the sound. The ease of our conversation had vanished and tension had built a brick wall between us. But the more he evaded my questions the more my curiosity grew, and the more I *needed* to know the answers. Why wouldn't he just tell me?

"It's just, I know your art," I said, before I could stop myself. "And that drawing seemed like it *meant* something."

He visibly tensed and one of his chopsticks snapped in his

hand. "Jesus, it's just a fucking drawing. You're reading way too much into it."

"Am I?"

He tossed the broken chopstick on the table and pushed his plate away. "It doesn't mean anything. I draw lots of people. Friends. Family. Random people on the street. That's all."

God, this had all gone horribly wrong. Hector was closed off about his emotions on even the best days, but I'd never seen him like this before. I had to back off. I didn't want to—I wanted to get *something* out of him. But I cared about Hector as a friend before anything else, and I could tell he desperately wanted me to drop this.

I plastered on a smile and made my voice light. "In that case, you should draw that guy over there in the Halo helmet and pink tutu and nothing else."

Hector laughed. I could tell it was forced, but at least things returned to some semblance of normality between us. Even if I couldn't shake the feeling that he'd been lying.

# CHAPTER FOUR
## HECTOR

In our dressing room, Jared bounced up and down on his heels and shook his hands out while doing his vocal exercises. I wanted to yell at him to sit down and shut up because he was making me crazy, but I couldn't mess with his pre-show ritual. That would only fuck things up for the entire band, and we were already on edge as it was.

Tonight was the first concert on *The Sound* tour, featuring the top four bands from the show. Our first performance in a giant stadium in front of over ten thousand people. We'd been rehearsing for the past week, from the minute *The Sound* had ended, but we'd had a lot to practice. Not just the songs either, but things like the order we played them in, the transitions between them, where Maddie and Jared stood on stage, even what Jared said to the audience—it was all scripted down to the second. We had so much to learn in a very short period of time, and that had resulted in some serious growing pains. We were used to that after the whirlwind that was *The Sound*, but I didn't think anything could really prepare a band for something as massive as this.

I wasn't nervous about tonight's show, not exactly. The waiting was what killed me. I wanted to get out there and play already, not sit around on my ass while two other bands went on before us.

Knowing Tara might be in the audience only made it worse.

I stretched my arms and neck, forcing myself not to check my phone again. It was almost time for our set and, as far as I knew, Tara still hadn't arrived. I had to accept that she wasn't coming. Not after what had happened at lunch.

After our fight—or whatever the hell that had been—I'd insisted on paying the bill, despite her protests, and told her I had to head to the stadium for the sound check. She'd promised she was coming to the concert, but I hadn't heard a single thing from her since then.

Thank god she'd only seen the one drawing. If she'd flicked through the rest of my sketchbook she'd think I was a stalker or something. I *did* have pictures of my other friends in there, too. Hell, I'd just done one yesterday of Maddie playing the guitar that Jared wanted to keep. But I had more drawings of Tara than anyone else. And like she'd said, they were different.

Whenever I missed her, or after we video chatted and her smile was still fresh in my mind, I had the urge to sketch her. Any strong emotion made me want to draw, to let it out through my art. Jared told me it was the same for him when he wrote music. And Tara always made me feel more than anyone else— no matter how hard I tried not to let her in.

But I'd never shown the drawings of Tara to anyone. There was something more...private about them. They were for me and no one else. She wasn't supposed to ever find out about them.

I broke down and checked my phone again. Nothing. Dammit.

"You okay?" Maddie asked from her spot on one of the couches, where she idly strummed her acoustic guitar. With her low-cut red top, black leather pants, and geeky glasses, she looked smoking hot, like some kind of sexy librarian.

"Yeah," I said, shoving the phone back in my jeans.

Jared sank beside Maddie, sliding an arm around her waist. The two of them had been joined at the hip ever since they'd officially become a thing during the finale of *The Sound*. Now they were completely unbearable 24/7, like five minutes apart would kill them. Don't get me wrong, I was happy for them. I just didn't want to see them making out every single minute of the day.

I'd been kind of a jerk to Maddie when I'd first met her. After Jared had nearly broken up our band by sleeping with Becca, our previous bassist, I'd told him I didn't want another girl to replace her. I'd thought Maddie was just another of his groupies, looking for an excuse to get in his bed. And like I'd predicted, the two of them had hooked up and nearly ruined our chances on *The Sound*.

But Maddie surprised me by being a great guitarist and, even with the drama, I grew to really like her. Not to mention, I realized how much Jared had changed because of her. He was better when she was around, happier than I'd seen him in years, and he obviously loved her. Now I couldn't imagine not having her in the band.

"Is Tara here yet?" Maddie asked.

"No. I don't think she's coming." I shrugged. "Whatever."

Jared arched an eyebrow. "I think Hector's not telling us something."

I glared at him. "*I* think you're annoying as hell."

"Aha! That means I'm right."

"Ooh," Maddie said, setting her guitar aside. "What do you think he's hiding?"

"I'm not hiding anything!"

"Something must have happened when they had lunch," Jared said. "He pouted all through the sound check."

"I did not."

Jared was usually so wrapped up in himself that it always

surprised me when he noticed shit like that. Then again, he knew me better than anyone, even Tara. Best friends were such a pain in the ass sometimes.

"No? You kept coming in a measure early on the 'Somebody Told Me' bridge. That's not like you."

Unfortunately, he was right. I'd been totally distracted during our sound check and it had thrown off the entire band. I needed to get my head together before we went on stage.

"Nothing happened."

"Is that the problem?" Maddie asked, her voice concerned. "You *wanted* something to happen with Tara?"

"No!" The way she looked at me implied she knew my secret, but until this week I'd never even mentioned Tara to Maddie. Not even Kyle knew how I felt about her. Only one person did. "Let me guess. Jared told you."

She gave me a sympathetic smile. "I think it's cute that you've loved her all this time. It explains a lot, too. Like how you never talk about girls. Or seem to notice they exist at all."

"I can't believe you," I growled at Jared. "That was private. You've broken the bro code, man."

He gave a slight shrug. "She figured it out. What was I supposed to do?"

"It was kind of obvious," she said, her fingers tangling with his. "How was it meeting her in person for the first time?"

"Weird."

"Uh huh…"

"And good." I looked away, my teeth grinding together. Why were we still talking about this? "But mostly weird."

The door opened and Kyle came in, wearing a hoodie over his dyed-black hair. His sleeves were rolled up, showing off the tattoos on each arm. He passed a bottle of water to each of us and plopped down on the other couch.

"Where's Hector's girl?" he asked.

"Shit, does *everyone* know?" I muttered.

"Pretty much."

"She's not coming."

"No way," Maddie said. "I saw how she smiled at you during your panel. She'll be here."

I grunted and crossed my arms, hoping that signaled the end of this conversation. Jared opened his mouth and I knew he was going to continue bugging me, but I was saved by a knock on the dressing room door.

Kyle hopped up and opened it. A security guard stood on the other side, one finger on his earpiece. "There's a blonde with a backstage pass who says she knows you guys, but she's not on the list."

I jumped to my feet before I realized what I was doing. "That must be Tara. You can send her in."

Maddie smiled. "Told you."

I paced back and forth, too restless to sit again. Now that she was here I wasn't sure what to say to her. How long would it be awkward between us after what happened at lunch? Maybe if I didn't bring it up we could both forget about it.

But when the door opened it wasn't Tara who stood there, but Becca, our former bassist.

After the way things had ended, Becca was just about the last person I'd expect to see in our dressing room. She looked better than she had the last time I'd seen her, when she'd gotten drunk, thrown a bottle at Jared's head, and quit the band. Her blue hair was light blond now, like she'd bleached it, and she seemed more awake or something.

Jared stood up quickly, his eyes narrowing. "What are you doing here?"

"Hey," Becca said, closing the door behind her. "I wanted to talk to you. Well, to the entire band."

Shit, I hoped she wasn't here to cause trouble. I glanced at Maddie to see if she was okay, but she looked more curious than upset. Even so, I stood up straighter, getting ready for a fight. Not a physical one, of course, but mentally preparing myself for whatever was about to go down. "Spit it out then."

She rolled her eyes. "Relax. I just came to say sorry. That's it."

"You want to say *sorry*?" Kyle asked.

Becca ruffled her short hair, looking at the floor. "Yeah, I'm sorry. For everything that happened with us, and for quitting the band when you needed me. Oh, and for what I said to that reporter while you were on *The Sound*. I was drunk and didn't realize he was recording it, and… yeah, that's no excuse. It was still shitty of me even if I was drunk."

"You drove all the way to San Diego to apologize to us?" I asked. It was a two or three hour drive from LA, where we all lived. Probably even more with Comic-Con traffic.

"I've been staying in San Diego with a friend since I got kicked out of my apartment last month. When I heard you were doing a show tonight I thought I'd stop by." We still must have looked skeptical because she sighed and continued. "Look, I stopped drinking and doing all that shit and I'm trying to get my life together. In a few days I'm heading to Dallas to live with my sister, maybe go back to college and start over. So I wanted to make sure we were cool before I left."

Jared didn't look convinced, but Maddie placed a hand on his arm. "It's all in the past," she said to Becca. "Don't worry about it."

The two of them stared at each other for long beat, and then Becca nodded. If there was any lingering resentment between them, neither of them showed it. I was surprised Maddie would be so forgiving, until I remembered her mother was a recovering alcoholic, too.

"We're cool," Jared said, all traces of hostility gone.

"Thanks for the apology," Kyle added.

I reluctantly nodded. She did seem sober, for once. I'd forgotten what sober Becca looked like. And if the other guys were over the whole thing, then so was I.

"Good." Becca's shoulders relaxed. "Sucks that you didn't win *The Sound*, but it seems like the band is taking off anyway." She flicked a thumb at the door. "I'm going to head out and watch the show."

"How'd you get a backstage pass, anyway?" I asked.

"I hooked up with one of the security guards a week or two ago. Guess he's still into me." She shrugged. Jared laughed, and the tension in the room eased.

He grabbed one of the flyers off the table and held it out to her. "We're having a party Saturday night. You should stop by."

If it were up to me, I'd suggest we all go our separate ways and never speak again. But maybe Jared still felt bad for what had gone down between them. Another sign that he'd changed; the old Jared would have kicked her out of our dressing room by now.

She pocketed the flyer. "Maybe I will. Thanks."

As soon as she left, we got the fifteen-minute warning. Time to exit our dressing room and head to the stage—but first, Jared pulled us all in for a band huddle.

He sucked in a deep breath before starting. "Tonight we're playing a sold out show in our biggest venue ever. Thousands of people are waiting for us to go on stage. Can we just let that sink in for a minute?"

We all went quiet and the enormity of what we were doing really hit me. "Oh shit," I said with a short laugh. "We are so screwed."

"We're still figuring some things out," Jared admitted. "But this tour is our dream. And for us to achieve it so fast…of course there are going to be some rough spots along the way."

"We practiced our asses off," Kyle said. "We've got this."

"I still can't believe this is really happening," Maddie said, with awe in her voice.

A slow smile spread across Jared's face. "It's happening. A few weeks ago we were playing frat parties, parking lot shows, and small clubs. Now we're playing massive stadiums across America. Somehow, we've become an arena band almost overnight."

Kyle shook his head, like he was shocked by it, too. "It's been an amazing journey, and it's only the beginning."

"I'm so happy I could be a part of it," Maddie added, sniffing.

"You guys are cheesy as hell," I said, grinning at the three of them.

"Admit it, you love our cheese," Jared said.

"I admit nothing." He was right though. I loved Jared and Kyle like my own brothers, and Maddie already felt like a little sister to me, too. Even if they got a bit sappy sometimes and made me want to roll my eyes at them.

They all looked like they expected me to say something too, to finish up our little bonding moment. I wasn't good at that stuff, but I cleared my throat and gave it a shot anyway. "Whatever happens, tonight will be great 'cause we're together. We're more than a band, we're a family."

"Aww," Maddie said, her big eyes watering behind her glasses.

"See? I knew you had some cheese in you, too." Jared slapped me on the back. "You big softie, you."

I donned my toughest face. "Hey, there's nothing about me that's soft."

"Is that so?" His eyebrows shot up as he glanced at my jeans.

Maddie laughed. "Tara is one lucky girl."

I groaned. Of course they'd bring this back to her again. "Nothing's going to happen with Tara. We're just friends."

"Hmm, where have I heard that before?" Kyle asked, looking pointedly at Maddie and Jared. They'd given us that line a dozen times before finally admitting that they were, in fact, much more than friends. But this thing with Tara was different.

"Nah. She's not even here."

"Oh, she's here," Kyle said, with a grin. "Alexis texted me a few minutes ago."

"What? She is?" Hot damn, she'd come to see me perform after all. Maybe the sketchbook incident hadn't freaked her out as much as I'd thought.

"Perfect," Jared said. "Now, let's get out there and put on the best show we can, and try to have some fun, too."

We broke the huddle and headed toward the stage. Knowing Tara was in the audience gave me a burst of energy. I couldn't wait to get out there and do this thing. With the others at my side I felt like we could take on the world together, one song at a time.

Shit, maybe I *was* just as cheesy as they were.

# CHAPTER FIVE
## TARA

As soon as I arrived at the stadium the clichés came back in force. My heart raced, my hands were clammy, and my inner goddess—whatever that was—awakened, all in anticipation of seeing Hector again. I'd become one of those girls I'd once mocked in books, who met the hot guy and instantly lost all common sense. Never again would I scoff at them.

I checked my face in my phone's camera. Was I too done up? Did I look like I was trying too hard? He'd seen me in pajamas and no makeup many times before. He'd seen me when I was so busy with school and our books that I forgot to take showers for days. He'd even seen me when I'd had the flu. Maybe I should take off some of this makeup. The eye shadow at least. I wasn't going on a date, after all, I was just watching my friend perform with his band. Not a big deal.

But it was too late, because I was already at the entrance to the stadium. Like everything at Comic-Con, there was a gigantic line to get in but I skipped past it using my backstage pass—thank you, Hector—and the security guard waved me inside. The crowd was massive, with high energy and excitement you couldn't help but feel under your skin. People cheered, music blared from the stage, and the air smelled vaguely of beer and popcorn. Everyone was with a group of friends or part of a couple. And then there was me, all by myself.

I checked my ticket and headed for my seat while Brazen, the band that had gotten third place on *The Sound*, did a Maroon 5 cover on stage. I wanted to find Hector backstage, but Villain Complex would be on soon and I couldn't miss their performance. My spot was crazy good too, right in the center of the front row. So close I could see up the Brazen's singer's skirt as she danced around.

My phone buzzed in my pocket. A text from Andy: *Want to have dinner?*

The sight of his name made my stomach clench. I reread his text over and over, surprised he'd contact me this soon after our break-up. We'd agreed to try to stay friends, but I wasn't sure either of us were ready for that yet.

I texted him: *Sorry, busy tonight.*

He wrote back: *Tomorrow?*

I hesitated with my fingers over the screen. Tomorrow Hector and I had a Black Hat Comics party, but after that he would probably be busy with his band. It might be uncomfortable to see Andy so soon, but it *would* be nice to not have to eat alone. Like me, he was by himself at Comic-Con and I could understand why he wanted to hang out. When you're surrounded by so many people it's even more noticeable how alone you are.

And the only reason he'd even come to Comic-Con was because of me. We'd bought the tickets months ago, and when we'd broken up it had been too late to refund them or cancel his flight. Instead, he'd found a cheap hotel room for himself since he couldn't stay in mine anymore.

*OK,* I replied. *Have party in evening but will text when over.*

*Perfect,* he wrote back. *See you then.*

I hated admitting it, but I was sad that Andy and I had broken up *before* Comic-Con instead of after. He'd been my plus one for everything for the past year, and before that it had been Sam, and before that another guy…

The truth was, I wasn't very good at being single. I liked having someone to go places with, who could make new experiences less awkward, who gave me a little confidence boost thanks to the knowledge I had someone familiar at my side. Andy had fit the bill perfectly.

I blamed growing up in a small town in Nebraska with five

brothers and sisters. I'd never done *anything* alone as a kid, had never had a second of time to myself. I'd done whatever I could to get some space from my family, but now I lived a paradox: being surrounded by people drained me and yet I hated being by myself, too.

Maybe that's why I spent so much of my free time talking to Hector online. He'd always made me feel less alone.

It was ridiculous. I was an adult, I should be able to do things by myself and not feel uncomfortable—but I did. Definitely something to work on in the future.

I'd have to get used to being alone soon, too. Other than Hector, all my friends were back in Boston. After graduating last month most of us were moving on, and I wasn't sure how many I'd keep in touch with in the future. We'd all promised to continue to be friends, but would we be anything more than social media acquaintances in a few months?

Once I moved to New York I'd have to make new friends, I supposed. I'd dreamed of working in publishing my entire life, so when I'd been hired to be part of the new comics division of Ostrich Books, one of the biggest publishers in the world, it had sounded like the ideal job. Yet, despite how perfect it seemed, I was hit with a massive wave of anxiety every time I thought about it. Probably because I didn't know anyone there or have a place to live yet.

Brazen finished and the audience cheered while the singer bounced off stage, holding the hand of her mentor from *The*

*Sound.* As soon as they were gone, a girl with fiery red curls dropped into the seat beside me and smiled. "Tara, right?"

"Yeah…" I studied her face. She looked familiar, with very pale skin, a hint of freckles across her nose, and pretty green eyes. She wore a leather jacket and had a fancy camera around her neck. "You're Alexis! Kyle's girlfriend!"

She laughed. "That's me."

"I saw you in the audience at the panel. And Hector's told me all about you."

"Did he? Interesting. He's been very secretive about you."

"Oh…well, I guess there's not that much to tell." I tried not to sound disappointed, but it stung that he didn't talk about me with his friends. Then again, why would he? I was just some girl he knew online, after all.

"That's definitely not true," Alexis said. "Hector's extremely private, even with his closest friends. The fact that he hasn't told us anything means you must be *very* important to him."

"I don't know about that…"

"I do." She leaned close, like she was whispering a secret. "In fact, Kyle said Hector's going crazy because he's worried you wouldn't come tonight."

"He is?" Did he think I was upset about the drawing? Even if I was (which I wasn't), how could he believe I wouldn't come tonight? I wouldn't miss this for anything. "Maybe I should text him…"

"They're already on their way to the stage. But don't worry, I told them you're here."

"Oh. Thanks." I tried to relax in my seat but excitement bubbled under my skin, making me almost jumpy. "I can't wait. I've never seen them play before. Except on TV, of course."

She checked her camera lens and adjusted something. "They're pretty impressive. Even before they were famous they were good, but being on the show made them even better. Maddie helped a lot, too. She brought the band together and made everything click."

"So you've known them a long time?" I vaguely remembered Hector saying something about Alexis and Kyle getting back together at the Battle of the Bands they'd competed in, but I didn't know much more than that.

"Since high school. Give or take a few years when I went away for college."

"Do you know when Hector last had a girlfriend?" I slapped a hand over my mouth, cheeks flaring hot. "Sorry, I don't know where that came from."

She hesitated, not meeting my eyes. "You'll have to ask him about that. But as far as I can tell, it's been a long time."

I nodded. It's not like it really mattered or was any of my business. But the not knowing still drove me crazy.

The lights dimmed and the entire crowd seemed to jump to its feet at once, including me. Fog crept across the stage and a red glow slowly illuminated the darkness. The stadium was silent except for the buzz of excitement, the anticipation for the band about to come out. My chest was tight, my breathing difficult, my heart a speeding train that threatened to derail at any moment.

Just when I thought I couldn't take any more of it, the room burst into sound with the opening of "Uprising" by Muse. The lights brightened, gradually revealing the band already on stage. Maddie on the right, her fingers flying across her guitar, the fake wind blowing her hair like in a music video. Kyle on the left, rocking out behind his keyboard, his black hair hanging in his eyes. And Jared in the middle, playing bass.

A spotlight flashed on him when he started singing. In person he was even more drop dead gorgeous than on screen, with his tattooed arms, sinful blue eyes, and naughty smile. His voice had a way of creeping into your very soul, and he had this crazy magnetism that made it nearly impossible to take your eyes off him. Especially when he wasn't playing and could grip the microphone like a lover and croon into it. No wonder so many ladies threw themselves at him.

But while everyone drooled over Jared, my eyes sought out Hector, who had gone shirtless tonight. It was harder to see him in the back, but I could still glimpse his muscular arms and shoulders while his drumsticks danced through the air. He was an animal, pounding against the drums like he was possessed by something, yet somehow never completely losing control.

The big screens beside the stage flashed between the different band members and showed Hector from behind, giving a shot of his smooth back, all those coiled muscles flexing and rippling while he played. Sweat slicked his arms as he poured himself into the music, his drumsticks moving fast yet never missing a beat. He was glorious. Strong. Powerful. And ridiculously sexy. I wanted to lick the sweat off him, which was sort of gross, but I didn't care. I'd do it to taste him, to explore that hard, muscular body with my tongue. And my hands. And every other part of me.

I couldn't deny it any longer. Meeting Hector in person had awakened something in me. I'd always found him hot, of course. And sure, I'd fantasized about him a few times, but I'd never seriously thought of him as anything more than a friend. He'd always been too far away, too off limits, too impossible to even consider. But now he was more than a daydream I tried desperately to ignore—he was a very tempting reality.

Once we'd come face to face a flick had been switched, and I felt something...more.

And seeing him play tonight? That made me *want* him.

For the rest of Villain Complex's set, Alexis and I bounced along to the songs, arms in the air, throwing ourselves into the music with everyone else in the crowd. The band played through all the covers they'd done on the show, plus their own song, "Behind the Mask." Their former mentor, Dan, even came out to do a cover of one of his band's songs with them. They finished with their sensual cover of "Bad Romance," making the audience go wild.

When the lights went up, I felt like I'd just had the greatest sex of my life. All that anticipation, the buildup of excitement, the rush of the music, and finally the climax at the end. I was exhausted yet almost giddy with exhilaration. I wanted to see them play again immediately.

"How is it possible they didn't win the show?" I asked Alexis.

"Tell me about it," she said. "Ready to go backstage, or do you want to watch the country princess and her band perform?"

She was referring to the band that had won *The Sound*, Fairy Lights, but even if I'd been a fan I couldn't wait a second longer to see Hector again. "I definitely want to go backstage."

Alexis led me out of the aisles to a security guard along the side who checked our passes and let us through. I followed on her heels through the dizzying maze of backstage areas, packed with roadies, equipment, and more security guards. She seemed to know where she was going, taking us down long brightly lit hallways and past doors labeled only with letters. Finally she knocked on a door that said C, and then opened it without waiting for a response.

Music hit me—the sound of an acoustic guitar being played and Jared's voice raised in song, followed by a chorus of laughter. We stepped into a large room with a giant TV on one wall, a mini-kitchen in the back, and two large brown leather couches that the band was sprawled across.

"Hey!" Kyle looked up from the beer he was sipping. He patted the seat next to him and Alexis slid into his arms, curling against his side like she belonged there.

Jared and Maddie were tangled together on the other couch. She sat on his lap and they held the guitar together, playing it at the same time, completely in their own world. When Jared starting singing again I recognized the song as "Howlin' For You" by the Black Keys.

Hector sat on his own, apart from the other two couples, his well-developed arms draped across the back of the couch. I was disappointed to see he'd put on a shirt after their set had ended.

He jumped to his feet as soon as he saw me. "Tara. You're here."

Maybe it was the way he smiled at me, like I was the best thing he'd seen all day. Maybe it was an echo of desire left over from seeing him perform. Maybe it was all the other love in the room. But suddenly I had the strongest urge to kiss him.

# CHAPTER SIX
## HECTOR

Tara hugged me, fitting against my chest like it was the most natural place for her to be. I circled my arms around her, relieved that she wasn't upset with me. And instantly hard, thanks to the lush, feminine curves of her body pressed against mine. Damn, I could get used to that.

Except I couldn't, because no matter what happened at Comic-Con, she was still going to live thousands of miles away from me. I had to keep that in mind at all times.

"You were incredible," she said, looking up at me from behind her long lashes. "Thanks for inviting me, and for the backstage pass."

"No problem," I said, forcing myself to pull away. "Hey everyone, this is Tara."

There wasn't much space on the couch so she had to sit close to me, setting me on alert for the chance we might accidentally touch. The others were all grinning madly, looking back and forth between the two of us. Shit, they'd better not embarrass me in front of her. Or say anything to tip her off about how I felt about her. Maybe bringing her backstage to meet them was a mistake. It had been so much easier when no one knew about her and that part of my life was completely separate from this one.

"I'm so happy to meet you," Maddie said to Tara, with a big smile. "I wanted to come to your signing but Hector was being a total grump about it. Do you think you could sign my copy of *Misfit Squad* now?"

Tara looked startled for a second, but then laughed. "Of course! I didn't know you were a fan."

"Maddie's a *huge* fan," Jared said. "I am, too. But then again, I'm a fan of everything Hector does." He winked at me and I rolled my eyes.

Maddie brought out her copy of *Misfit Squad*, which I'd given her while we were on *The Sound*. She'd read it over the past week between rehearsals and had gushed over it constantly, asking me a million questions about what was going to happen next. She'd already made me sign it and now she handed it to Tara, who pulled out one of her metallic pens.

"I feel so weird signing this," Tara said as she opened the book up. "Like I should be asking for your autograph instead. I watched you all on TV every week and it's kind of intimidating to actually meet you in person."

Alexis groaned. "Don't tell them that. You'll make their egos even bigger."

"My ego is the perfect size, thank you very much," Jared said, grinning like a lazy cat. "Just like every other part of me."

I threw a pillow at Jared's head. "Dude, no one needs to know that. Except Maddie."

"Oh, she knows." He waggled his eyebrows and Maddie actually blushed. That made Tara laugh, and I relaxed a little at the sound.

"Thanks so much," Maddie said, when Tara handed the book back to her. "I keep trying to bribe Hector into giving me an early copy of the second one or give me some hints or *something*, but he refuses."

"I don't have any copies yet," I said. "And you know I don't give out spoilers."

"Hector *is* crazy about the no-spoilers-thing," Kyle said.

"They just really annoy me, that's all," I muttered.

"Forget him," Tara said to Maddie, in a low voice like they were conspiring together. "I'll hook you up. As long as you answer a few burning questions I have about the show."

Maddie grinned. "Deal. What do you want to know?"

"First, did it hurt when you fell off the stage?"

"It was more shocking than painful, though I did twist my ankle pretty bad." Maddie and Jared shared a small smile, as though they were both in on a secret. "But it led to Jared kissing me for the first time, so it was worth it."

"*That's* when you two got together?" I asked.

"Yep. In the elevator." Jared kissed Maddie on the neck. "And back in her hotel room. And…"

Kyle raised a tattooed hand to stop him. "We get the idea."

Tara asked a few more questions about the show, and then my friends asked her about writing *Misfit Squad* and going to college in Boston. I'd worried she'd feel out of place as the new person in the group, but it wasn't awkward at all. In fact, she seemed to fit right in.

We all discussed our plans for the next few days at Comic-Con and Jared handed Tara a flyer for our party on Saturday night. I'd designed it myself and it read "Villain Afterparty," with silhouettes of famous villains like Loki, Catwoman, and Magneto on a red background. The party was taking place in a club inside our hotel and promised drinks, costume contests, karaoke, and more. Across the bottom it said, "Wear your most villainous costume!"

"Sounds fun," Tara said. "Are you dressing up, Hector?"

Jared grinned. "Hell yeah he is."

I scowled at him. "I don't want to, but Jared and Maddie love this shit."

Tara nudged me with her shoulder. "Let me guess, Red Power Ranger?"

"What? That doesn't even fit the villain theme." I couldn't believe she would even bring that up.

"No, but it'd be hilarious."

"Hey, just 'cause I loved that show as a kid doesn't mean I'd dress up as one of them."

"We're all going as Batman villains," Maddie said, saving me from further embarrassment. "My roommate Julie designs the most amazing costumes and she made them for us. We're entering the Masquerade, too."

The Masquerade was the annual costume contest at Comic-Con. Julie planned to enter us as a group in the hopes of winning one of the many prizes and to show off her creations in front of thousands of people.

Cosplay was not my thing at all and I'd only agreed to be part of it to make Maddie and Jared happy. Not that I *really* minded dressing up, but hey, I had to keep up my tough guy act.

"Cool theme." Tara turned toward me. "So what's your costume?"

"They're making me go as Bane."

"Ooh. I want to see you all dressed up. I'll try to make it."

Maddie's eyes widened behind her black-rimmed glasses. "You should totally dress up with us. I bet Julie could whip up something quickly for you."

I gave Maddie a *back off* look. "She doesn't need to dress up if she doesn't want to."

"No, of course not. Sorry, I wasn't trying to pressure you, Tara."

"It's okay," she said, smiling. "I'd love to join you guys. I have a costume for tomorrow's Black Hat party I could use, but going as a group sounds a lot more fun."

"Oh, yay!" Maddie clapped her hands together. "Hmm, which Batman villain could you be?"

Jared tilted his head and considered. "Talia Al Ghul is the other big female villain in Batman."

"True, but she doesn't have a distinct, recognizable costume."

"Good point. Ah, I have an idea!" He whispered something into Maddie's ear and her face lit up.

"Yes! I'll text Julie now so she can start preparing! This is going to be good."

"What's happening?" Tara asked me, resting a hand on my bicep as she leaned closer.

I shook my head. "It's best to just let them do their thing when they get like this. No one can stop them."

She laughed and Maddie eyed us closely. She tugged on Jared's shirt. "We should go back to the hotel and let Hector and Tara catch up."

He nuzzled against her neck. "I like the sound of that."

Jared and I were sharing my room, which had been provided by Black Hat Comics, while Maddie was staying with her two roommates in a different hotel down the street. Unfortunately that meant they kept trying to get me out of the room so they could fool around. It sounded like I'd be locked out of the room for a while tonight. Lucky me.

Jared stood up, and he and Kyle shared one of those looks where they seemed to communicate telepathically. They'd always done that and it could be annoying as hell sometimes. Like now, when I wondered what they were up to—at least, until Jared patted me on the shoulder, discreetly slipping me a handful of condoms with a wink. Fucking typical of him.

Kyle nodded and hopped up from the couch, pulling Alexis with him. They had their own hotel room, since Alexis was working as a photographer while at Comic-Con. "We're going to head out too," he said. "We'll see you guys tomorrow."

They all rushed out of the room like it was on fire, leaving me and Tara alone on the couch, still sitting close from when there had been too many people on it.

Neither of us moved apart. Our eyes locked and it struck me again how pretty she was. Her soft lips twitched up into the slightest hint of a smile before she looked away, almost like she was shy or nervous.

I was hit by the overwhelming urge to draw her. I just hoped she wouldn't take it the wrong way. Or read too much into it.

"Stay like that." I grabbed my sketchbook off the other table and sat beside her again, just as close. She still didn't inch away.

She tilted her head. "Like what?"

"Don't move. I want to draw you."

She laughed and tucked a piece of golden hair behind her ear, folding her legs beneath her. "I'm all sweaty and tired and gross after a long day at Comic-Con."

"You look beautiful." The words slipped out by accident, but her warm smile made me not regret them. "I want to capture you just like this, on the day we finally met in person."

"What do I do?"

I took my pencil from the corner of the sketchbook and opened to a blank page. "Just act normal. Tell me what you most want to see at Comic-Con."

"Um, I don't know. The usual stuff. The Marvel and DC panels, but I've heard those are hard to get into." She shifted awkwardly, like she was trying to get comfortable but was too self-conscious now that she knew I was drawing her.

"We're camping out all night in the Hall H line tomorrow so we can get into them." I started my sketch, focusing on her cobalt blue eyes first. I couldn't capture them properly with just a black pencil, but I would do my best.

"Oh yeah?" She put her hands on the couch for a second, then moved them to her lap, like she couldn't decide what to do with them.

"We've got sleeping bags and food and beer. It'll be one big party. You should join us."

"That sounds fun. I might have to take you up on that."

She slowly relaxed as she told me about the things she'd

heard would be revealed at the DC and Marvel panels about the upcoming movies. I kept her talking as I sketched her smile, her bright eyes, the feminine curves of her face, the trail of blond hair down her shoulder, the delicate slope of her neck.

"I want to go to a couple different book panels tomorrow," she continued. "There's one with a bunch of bestselling fantasy and sci-fi authors that sounds amazing. Then in the afternoon there's a panel about writing and drawing diverse characters that I can't miss."

"I saw that in the schedule. It looked good."

"We should go together!"

I grinned, pleased that she wanted to spend so much time with me this week. "We will. Although we should have been *on* that panel."

She laughed. "True. You can complain to Miguel that he didn't hook us up."

"Nah. The less I have to talk in front of people, the better."

"I thought that stuff didn't make you nervous?"

"It doesn't. But I still hate it."

I stopped to examine my work. For the first time I felt like I was able to capture her, the *real* her, now that I'd finally met her in person.

"Are you done?" she asked, trying to sneak a peek.

"Mostly."

I could tweak the thing forever, but it was good enough to show her. Still, I hesitated, taking a moment to add a little more shading to her hair. She'd seen hundreds of my sketches before, along with that other drawing of her, but this one felt more important than anything else I'd done.

"Can I see?" She inched closer to me, her hip nudging against my side.

I relented, unable to deny her anything when she was this close. She gasped as soon as she saw the drawing. "Hector, this…this is beautiful."

"You like it?"

"I *love* it. I want to hug it to my chest, that's how much I love it, but I'm worried I'll smear it." She smiled down at my drawing before setting it beside her on the couch. "I'll just hug you instead."

Then she was in my arms again, soft, warm, and curvy, and I wrapped myself tight around her. This time neither of us pulled away. Instead, she smoothed her hands along my chest and looked up at me, her rose-colored lips parting. As I stared at her mouth I was tempted to do the thing I'd dreamed about for so long.

I'd never seen a more beautiful girl than her. Never wanted a girl more. Other women had been easy to resist. Jared had lured many of them away, and the rest weren't difficult to turn down. But not her. She was my weakness.

When she didn't move back, even after the reasonable time had passed for a friendly hug, courage flared in me. I bowed my head and brushed my lips across hers, the softest, lightest touch in case she didn't want this kiss. I expected her to pull away, to ask, "What are you doing?"

But she didn't.

She let out a quiet sigh, barely audible against my mouth, and closed her eyes like she was waiting for more. I took that as my cue and gave her another kiss, a real kiss this time. I was still hesitant, half-convinced she would stop me at any moment. This was crossing the line beyond friendship. I wasn't sure I should be doing it, but I couldn't help myself either. I'd dreamed of kissing Tara for years and now it was finally happening.

And impossibly, amazingly, she kissed me back.

I'd kissed girls before, but it had never been like this. Kissing Tara was like being kissed for the first time. Her lips were so sweet I wanted to taste her all night. I eased her mouth open softly, sliding my tongue inside, still waiting for her to stop me. I did everything slowly, giving her the opportunity to end it. But she didn't.

I kissed her deeper. Harder. Demanding more from her.

And she let me.

Then she kissed *me*, shifting so she was on her knees on the couch and leaning against my chest, almost in my lap. She clutched my face and I drew her in closer, gripping her waist, her breasts rubbing against me through our clothes. My hands dipped down to cup her ass, to slide along her curves for the first time.

I'd suffered through years of lusting after her and now I

finally had her in my arms. I couldn't stop myself. I wanted, *needed* to touch her everywhere. I had to explore her and see if she lived up to the fantasy in my head. Except after that kiss I knew she would be even better than anything I'd imagined.

When we finally broke apart she whispered my name and it had never sounded so good. "Are you sure those drawings mean nothing?" she asked.

I tensed up, completely caught off guard. "What?"

"I…forget it." She shook her head, pulling back. "God, what are we even doing?"

I drew in a ragged breath. "Do you want to stop?"

"Maybe…maybe we should."

It was hard to stop touching her, so fucking hard, but I lifted my hands off her. "Whatever you want."

She slowly climbed off the couch and yanked down her shirt, which had ridden up to show off her smooth, pale stomach. She looked dazed, like she wasn't sure what to do. "I…I should go. Before this goes any further."

I stood, but didn't say anything. I wasn't sure how to convince her to stay. Wasn't even sure I wanted her to stay.

No, that was a lie, as evidenced by my raging hard-on. I was dying for her to stay.

She walked to the door, but once there she paused and turned around. I took a step closer, unable to resist her magnetic pull. She stared at me and I was hypnotized by the way her breasts rose and fell with each of her quickened breaths. I moved even closer, until I was only an inch in front of her. Still, she didn't leave. It was almost like she *wanted* me to stop her.

Did she?

"The drawings do mean something," I confessed.

Her eyes widened. "What do they mean?"

I reached up to cup her face with my hands. My fingers were too big and unwieldy, too rough for her perfect, soft skin, yet I wanted to touch her everywhere.

"That I've been dying to kiss you for years."

I captured her mouth with mine again, showing her exactly how much the drawings meant.

And she kissed me back even harder.

# CHAPTER SEVEN
## TARA

Hector's kisses nearly undid me. I knew I should go, that this could only lead to trouble, but I couldn't. My body simply refused.

I couldn't resist him.

I didn't *want* to resist him.

He nipped at my lips and moved to kiss my neck, just below my ear. "Jesus, you have no idea how long I've thought about doing this."

I closed my eyes as his mouth continued down to my shoulder. "How long?"

"For as long as I've known you."

His confession shook me to my core. All this time, he'd desired me and I'd never known. If I had, would it have changed anything over the past three years? Would I have stayed with Andy for so long? Would I have taken the job in New York? I wasn't sure of anything anymore.

All I knew was that once I felt his lips on mine I needed more.

"What else have you wanted to do?" I asked.

"Tara..." He broke away and studied me with those smoldering brown eyes.

I dug my fingers into his shirt and pulled him closer, pressing myself against his hard chest. "Tell me."

"I want to see you naked. I want to taste every inch of you. I want to bury myself inside you." His voice was rough, like his words were strained. Like it was hard for him to speak. "I want you. *All* of you."

I felt drunk and out of control, all my inhibitions flying out the door. But I wasn't drunk, or not on alcohol at least. I was drunk on Hector, on hearing him speak to me like that. It was a powerful thing, knowing someone had desired you for years in secret.

And, if I was honest with myself, deep down I'd always desired him, too.

"Do it," I whispered. "Do everything you've thought about all this time."

His eyes blazed with lust and he pushed me against the door

I'd been about to leave through, pressing my back against it. His hands gripped my face, directing me, tilting my head exactly the way he wanted as he kissed me. His mouth was demanding, his grip strong, his desire rock hard against my waist. And I loved every second of it.

He raised his arms and pulled his shirt over his head, giving me a glorious view of his chest and abs. His body was all muscle and I wanted to trace every contour. I pressed a hand on his broad chest and slowly slid down, feeling each groove of his abs under my fingers, trailing along the dark hair from his waist into his jeans. They hung low on his defined hips, and the top of his briefs teased me with the promise of what was underneath. I wanted to explore that area so bad, but not yet. I moved my hands back up, to touch the rest of his strong body, to circle his dark nipples, to wrap my fingers around those firm biceps I'd been dying to touch. They felt as good as they looked, so firm and powerful and masculine.

He watched me explore him with an expression that looked almost...concerned. Like he was worried about something. With a body like that he had nothing to worry about. How was he still single? I know most girls fell all over Jared, but were they *blind*?

"You're gorgeous," I said.

He grunted. "That word doesn't apply to me. To you, hell yes. But not to me."

"Don't argue with me," I teased.

I slid my hands around his neck and pulled him down to my mouth, kissing him roughly. His fingers slipped under the lower hem of my shirt, sneaking across my bare skin, sliding up, up, up. We broke apart long enough for him to yank off my shirt and toss it on the floor, and then we were kissing again, like we couldn't stand to not be connected for even a second.

He pulled back and spun me around before I knew what was happening. My palms lay flat on the door, my breasts pressed against it, my head forced to the side. He unhooked my bra and let it drop, then ran his fingers across my naked back, making me shiver. As I whimpered, he shifted my hair to the side and kissed along the curve of my neck and down my spine. His hands pinned mine to the door, and all I could do was stand there and let him explore me with his mouth. He was so gentle it made me tremble, even as he roughly held my wrists in place. I'd never had a guy do this before, be both so tender yet so firm and demanding all at once. The combination turned me on more than I'd ever thought possible.

I arched against him, feeling how hard he was even through our clothes. "Hector, please."

He released one of my hands and I heard the scrape of fabric and the sound of his jeans hitting the floor behind me. A second later I felt him from behind, without those layers of clothes between us. Only my own clothes stopped our bodies from rubbing against each other.

He was naked behind me and I couldn't see him. I wanted to

turn around so bad, but he still held me in place. "Please," I begged again. "I need to see you."

He relented and turned me around, but before I got a chance to look at him he kissed down my chest and popped one of my breasts into his mouth. I moaned and clutched his broad shoulders for support as he sucked on my nipples, one and then the other. I still had a hard time believing this was happening, a part of me convinced that at any moment I'd wake up from this impossible dream and find myself alone in bed. There was a niggling voice in the back of my head that said this could never work and I should stop it before one—or both—of us got hurt, but it was easy to ignore as Hector's tongue swirled around my nipple.

Only when he'd completely worshipped both breasts did he pull away. Finally I was able to take him in, and naked Hector did not disappoint. His entire body was an ode to masculinity, like he was one of those Greek God sculptures, all nude and glorious. Every inch of his body was big and hard and powerful.

Oh yes. *Every* inch.

I wrapped my fingers around his length, needing to feel him in my hand. He groaned and tossed his head back, and I loved seeing what I did to him with the slightest touch. I wasn't normally this bold with a guy I'd just met, but then again, we weren't exactly strangers, were we? I'd known him for years, even if I'd only thought of him as a friend until now. Tonight he'd brought out something reckless and wild in me between his performance on stage, his demanding kisses, and his confession of desire, and I wanted more, more, more.

I let him go to undo my own jeans and lower them to the floor while he watched. I slowly stripped off all my clothes, until we both stood naked in front of each other. I hoped he liked what he saw.

He sucked in a breath. "Damn girl, you're even sexier in person than in my naughtiest fantasies about you."

His words made me warm and wet all over. I gripped his hips and dragged him toward me, and he took the hint. As he backed me against the door I raised one of my legs, trying to give him access, practically begging him to slip inside.

"Not yet," he said. "I have one more thing on my list first."

He slid down my body, his hands and mouth working me over together, moving lower, to my breasts, to my stomach, and even lower, to my hips, and *still* lower, spreading my legs apart. Of course—he'd listed three things he wanted to do to me. He'd seen me naked and now he was moving on to number two: tasting me all over.

I trembled when he sank to his knees and pressed his lips to my upper thigh, realizing he was about to go down on me right there where I was standing. He hooked one of my legs over his shoulder and his hands cupped my butt to support me. He teased me at first, kissing everywhere but where I wanted, building up the desire until I thought I would explode just from the anticipation alone. He ran his tongue along me slowly and I felt every inch of what he did like fire lapping along my body. I closed my eyes and leaned back against the door, weaving my fingers into his thick, curly hair, using my grip to steady myself as he continued his delicious torment.

He flicked his tongue against me, rubbing back and forth, sucking and licking. I spiraled higher and higher until I thought my legs would give out, but he held me up with his strong arms and I knew he wouldn't let me fall. I let go of any lingering fear about what we were doing and gave in to his adoration. My fingers tightened in his hair, my legs trembled uncontrollably, and my every nerve burst with pleasure that never seemed to end.

When it did, an eternity later, Hector unhooked my leg from around him and set it down. He stood slowly, his naked body rubbing along mine, and when he kissed me I tasted myself in his mouth.

"That's two out of three," he said. "One more to go."

While I recovered, he ripped open a condom and eased it along himself. He was going to take me right there, right against the door where he'd just gone down on me, and I was relieved because I didn't want to wait even the short amount of time it would take to get to the couch. And because having sex with a rock star against his dressing room door was hotter than anything I'd ever experienced before.

He grabbed my thighs and hefted me up with one quick, powerful movement, spreading my legs around him, bringing his body against mine at exactly the right height. I held onto his strong arms as he positioned us, lining up our bodies, and felt him nudging against me.

"This is the last chance to back out," he said. "To go back to the way things were before."

I tightened my legs around his hips to show I was just as eager as he was. "I'm not going anywhere."

With those words he thrust inside me, pinning me hard against the door. I cried out as he filled me, stretching my body in the most amazing way. I tightened my fingers around his biceps as he held me up, his large hands gripping my butt as he moved in and out of me with strong, powerful strokes.

I opened for him, accepting everything he gave me, letting myself become his completely. He was an animal as he pounded into me, straddling the line between creating a steady tempo and losing all control, just like when he played the drums. I couldn't get enough of this rough, demanding Hector, and my already sensitive body responded eagerly to him.

His smooth chest rubbed against my breasts as he hammered into me, making the door bang with each thrust. I let the passion he stirred take over as he created a relentless beat with our bodies. I slid up and down on him, taking him deeper, my knees gripping his waist while I grinded myself along to his movements. The friction built between my legs and Hector's grunts made me even more excited. I cried out so hard my throat became raspy, my body clenching around him as I came for a second time that night. He rammed his desire home inside me and moments later released himself with a long groan.

He stilled against me, but didn't put me down yet. We kissed each other softly, our bodies joined and twitching with the last echoes of pleasure. The rest of the room came back in focus: the hard wood of the door at my back, the cool air from the vents above us, the muffled sound of music in the distance.

As our heartbeats slowed, he pressed his forehead against mine. "I'm sorry. I couldn't hold back. Not after wanting you for so long."

"Don't apologize. I wanted you just as bad."

"It's been a while since I've been with anyone. Next time it will be better." He looked away, his eyebrows pinching together. "I mean, if there is a next time."

I gripped his chin and forced him to look at me. "Hector, that was the best sex I've ever had."

"It was?"

"God, yes. I wish you'd told me you wanted me sooner."

"You were with Andy. Now you're not."

He gave me one last lingering kiss before carrying me to the couch. My head spun as I lay there, my body tingling and pulsing all over. I'd never had sex standing up before. Andy had been great in bed, but he would never have been able to do it.

Hector was strong enough to hold me up throughout all of it. I didn't know how he could still stand after what we'd just done. He barely even seemed tired. His muscles were gleaming with sweat, but otherwise he didn't seem anywhere near as wiped out as I was. I couldn't take my eyes off his body. I'd never been with anyone so…big before. So hard and strong, all six foot whatever of rippling masculinity and dark, smooth muscle. God, I was a lucky girl.

He brought us a blanket and curled up behind me on the couch, his warm, naked body tucking around mine. It was a tight fit, but neither of us seemed to mind. He ran a finger along the chain at my neck, down to the amethyst at the end. My birthstone.

"You're wearing the necklace I got you." He sounded surprised.

"I never take it off."

Hector had mailed it to me for my twenty-first birthday. I was allergic to gold, so he'd had to special order one in sterling silver. It had meant a lot to me that he'd remembered.

I relaxed against him as he kissed my shoulder and draped an arm across my waist. My fingers idly traced the dark hair on his forearm. "How come you don't have any tattoos, like Jared and Kyle do?"

I felt him shrug behind me. "I've thought about it, but never came up with anything I'd want on my body for the rest of my life. I designed some of the guys' tattoos though, like the dragon and phoenix ones on Kyle's arms."

"Those are so cool. I should get you to design something for me."

"You? I can't see you with a tattoo."

I laughed. "No, I guess not. But if you designed it, maybe…"

His lips brushed the side of my neck. "I'll draw you anything you want."

"Maybe something to celebrate the publication of *Misfit Squad*? I always swore I'd get a tattoo when my first book came out."

"For that I might be tempted to get one with you. Although my *abuelita* would kill me if she found out."

"You'd have to get it somewhere your grandmother couldn't see it."

He chuckled, low and deep against my back, and we discussed what kind of tattoos we could get together. The more we talked about it, the more I wanted one.

"If we had time this week I'd take you to the place the guys got all their tattoos from." He traced lazy circles along my shoulder with his thumb. "You'll have to visit me in LA sometime. Although I'm sure there are plenty of good tattoo parlors in New York, too."

His words were like an electric jolt, clearing my head. Oh god, what had we done?

We'd definitely crossed over the "just friends" line but…into what? No matter how mind-blowing the sex had been, we still lived thousands of miles apart. Would he want a long-distance relationship? Or did he just see this as a quick fling during Comic-Con?

I didn't know if I was even ready for something more than

that. I'd just graduated college, gotten out of a long-term relationship, and wasn't sure where I'd be living in a month. My entire life was in flux. I couldn't handle yet another complication right now.

But how could it ever be the same between us after what we'd done?

Did I even *want* it to be the same?

I wasn't sure.

All I knew was that we had to figure it out before things went any further.

Except my eyes were so heavy and he felt so good around me, behind me, against me. I couldn't bear to bring it up yet. We would have to discuss this soon…but for now I just wanted to enjoy this moment a tiny bit longer.

# CHAPTER EIGHT
# HECTOR

I'd thought nothing could be better than being inside Tara, but having her fall asleep in my arms? That was pretty fucking fantastic, too.

I wasn't sure how long we stayed curled up together on the couch under a shared blanket, drifting in and out of sleep. At some point she turned to face me, nuzzling against my neck and melting further into my arms. I wrapped myself around her and let myself slip away.

Until the door opened with a loud click, jolting us both awake.

We sat up, confused, and Tara scrambled to cover herself

with the blanket. I shifted in front of her, blocking her from view of whoever had barged in on us.

A woman stood at the door in a uniform, with a cart of cleaning supplies. She took one look at our naked, entwined bodies and flushed. "So sorry," she said. "I thought the room was empty. I'll come back later."

The door shut behind her and Tara put a hand to her head. "What time is it?"

I grabbed my phone from my jeans, which were in a pile on the floor. "Fuck. It's five in the morning."

"Oh god. Last night...." She blinked sleep from her eyes. "I mean, it was amazing, but..."

Yeah.

*But.*

Jesus, I'd let things get way out of control. Tara was never supposed to know how I felt about her. I'd resolved to never let her get that close, to never let *anyone* in like that again. But I'd been so overwhelmed by her sheer presence I hadn't been able to help myself.

We sat face forward on the couch, neither of us looking at each other. It was like we'd forgotten how to talk now that we'd had sex. One thing was obvious: we couldn't go back to the ways things were before Comic-Con.

"What are we going to do?" she finally asked.

"I don't know."

"Do you want...." She chewed on one of her fingernails, like she often did when she was nervous. "Do you want to—"

I cut her off. "To get some breakfast? Yeah, I'm starving."

"That's...not what I was going to ask."

She looked so serious, but I couldn't have this discussion right now. Or ever. "Tara—"

"Do you want to talk about last night?" she blurted out.

"No. I really don't."

"Why not?"

"Isn't that talking about it?" I tugged on my jeans, feeling way too exposed sitting there buck naked beside her. I should tell her...something. Not that I loved her, hell no, but that she looked beautiful this morning or that last night was amazing, or something, *anything*. But there was a tightness in my throat that I couldn't seem to get words around. I didn't know what to say. I had no fucking clue what we should do next.

"I know this whole thing is kind of crazy," she said, slowly. "Andy and I just broke up, and you and I have been friends forever and we don't want to mess that up, especially since we still have to work together, and then there's the distance problem..."

It sounded like she thought the whole thing was a mistake. Maybe it was. I lived in LA and she was moving to New York and there was no future for us. When Comic-Con ended she'd be leaving me behind. Like my parents. Like Amanda. I wasn't going through that shit again.

"I can't do long distance," I said.

"Oh. I just thought, maybe…" She drew in a long breath and stood, clutching the blanket to her chest. "So what are we going to do? Go back to being friends? Try to forget last night ever happened?"

Like I could ever forget last night. I'd always remember the way she'd moaned and gripped my arms. The feel of being sheathed inside her. The taste of her on my tongue. I wished I didn't know those things, but I did and I would never be the same.

I grabbed my shirt from the corner. "Whatever you want."

"But what do *you* want?"

"I don't know!"

"God, Hector, just talk to me! Tell me what you want from me!"

"I don't want anything from you!"

She flinched, like I'd hit her, and I instantly regretted my words. That had been way harsh. I hadn't meant it the way it had sounded, but I didn't know how to smooth things over either.

She gathered her clothes off the floor while covering her breasts with one arm. She tried to put her bra on but had a hard time, like her hands were trembling. I started to move forward to help her but stopped myself. I got the feeling she didn't want me to get any closer.

"Tara…"

"No, I understand perfectly now. It was just sex, right?" She finished dressing and snatched her shoes. "Fine. It doesn't have to be anything more than that."

At the door she hesitated like she was waiting for me to say something. But I'd stopped her from leaving last night, and in the end it had backfired on me. I should never have drawn her or kissed her, should never have revealed how much I wanted her.

I turned away. "Yeah. It was just sex."

The door opened and closed with a click. She was gone.

I slumped down on the couch and my head dropped into my hands. I waited there for an hour in case she came back. Wishing I could rewind time and go back to before I had fucked everything up.

But she didn't return.

I got back to my hotel room and hopped in the shower without a word to Jared, who was still in bed, alone. Maddie must have returned to her room already. Good, one less person to deal with.

The hot water washed away all physical traces of last night but couldn't erase the memories. My mind was stuck on a loop, replaying this morning and trying to figure out how I could've handled things better. I came up with a thousand better responses to Tara's questions now that it was hours later, but that only made me even more miserable.

Because it hadn't just been sex. It had been so much more.

When I got out of the shower, Jared was making a cup of tea using hot water from the room's tiny coffee maker. He wore a t-shirt with Freddy Krueger on it and gave me an appraising look. "Long night?"

"Leave me alone," I muttered, rubbing my hair with a towel.

His eyebrows shot up. "Good morning to you, too. I'll make you some coffee."

I plopped onto the bed. "Don't bother. I'm going back to sleep."

He ripped open a packet of honey and poured the entire thing into his tea. For his voice, he always said. "You can't go back to sleep. People are already lining up outside the convention center to get in."

"I don't care."

"It's Comic-Con. You can't spend your entire day in the hotel room."

"Fuck off. I can do whatever I want." I was being a total asshole but I couldn't help it. Everyone wanted to talk, talk, talk, and I just wanted to be left the fuck alone.

"What the hell is going on with you?"

"I don't want to fucking talk about it!"

He threw up his hands. "Okay, chill."

He dropped into the chair behind the desk, playing on his phone while drinking his tea. For a few minutes I lay there with my eyes closed, but my mind wouldn't shut up. Regret and anxiety created a sick feeling in my gut that I couldn't get rid of. I rubbed my face, then dug out my phone to check if Tara had texted me. Yeah, right.

"Last night's show went pretty well," Jared suddenly said, almost as if to himself. He leaned back and propped his booted feet up on the desk. "Although I think we should add some lights behind the Villain Complex logo so it stands out more."

He continued on about how we could improve our performance for our next shows on the tour, but I knew he didn't expect me to reply. It was his way of letting me wallow for a while and showing he wasn't pissed at me for snapping at him. And something about his steady voice droning on about the band made me feel a little better.

"Though I never expected Becca to show up in our dressing room," he said, with a short laugh.

I'd missed whatever had led to that comment, but now I sat up, head spinning. My situation with Tara was not that different from Jared and Becca's. They'd been friends with a working relationship who'd had one night of sex they'd regretted the next morning. After that, things fell apart between them until Becca left the band, and then they never spoke again. Until last night, anyway.

Would something like that happen with me and Tara? We were better friends than Jared and Becca had ever been and we'd known each other a lot longer, but that didn't mean we weren't heading for the same fate.

"If you'd known Becca was going to leave the band, would you still have hooked up with her?" I asked.

Jared frowned, but didn't look up from his phone. "I wasn't really thinking straight when it happened. But what does it matter? It worked out in the end, and we got Maddie instead."

"That's not what I meant."

Jared put down his phone and studied me. "What are you really asking?"

"I don't know." I gave up on going back to sleep and started making myself some coffee. "Do you think you and Becca could ever be friends again?"

"I'm not sure. Before yesterday I would have said no chance in hell. Even now, I don't think we'll ever be friends, but as least there won't be any bad blood between us. Which is why I invited her to the party tomorrow."

I stared off into space while the coffee maker gurgled. They'd patched things up, but they were both moving on with their lives and would probably never speak again. Would that happen to us, too? Would Tara and I both drift apart to separate lives? It seemed likely, with the band gaining popularity and her new job.

I didn't want our friendship to be over. Or to stop collaborating with her on *Misfit Squad* and future books. But I didn't know if I could repair the damage to our relationship after what had gone down.

I didn't notice the coffee maker had finished until Jared moved to my side. He added two sugars the way I liked before handing the paper cup to me. "Becca and I were never as close as you and Tara. I don't think you need to worry." He coughed. "You know, *if* something like that ever happened to you."

I wasn't sure I liked this new, perceptive Jared. He seemed to have figured out the whole story without me even telling him. Damn best friends. I scowled but took the coffee from him. "Thanks."

He grabbed his wallet and slipped it in his jeans. "I'm meeting Maddie and Kyle for breakfast, then we're going to some panel on movie scores. You can come if you want. Or stay here. But you shouldn't waste a day of Comic-Con moping in your room."

As much as I hated to admit it, he was right. I'd never be able to sleep and would just make myself crazy lying in bed thinking about Tara. I could hit the gym and try to work some energy off, but then what? Sit around, driving myself insane until the party tonight? Get drunk and try to forget?

"Fine. I'm in." Hanging out with my friends would distract me from obsessing over Tara, if nothing else. I'd force myself to put her out of my mind completely.

Until the party tonight, when I'd have to face her again.

# CHAPTER NINE
## TARA

I should have been having fun. It was Friday at Comic-Con and there were a million things to do and see and each one was better than the last.

But all I could think about was Hector.

As I wandered the exhibit hall alone (yes, I was trying to get better about that) everything reminded me of him. A woman dressed as Cruella de Vil brought to mind his friends and their villain-themed party. An artist doing a live sketch awakened memories of Hector's drawings of me. A poster for a sci-fi TV show made me recall the times we'd watched it "together." I'd had to record each episode and wait to watch it since I was three hours ahead of him, but it was worth it to hear his snarky live commentary, which always made me laugh.

I couldn't even *look* at the Black Hat Comics booth, where our book was prominently on display. Especially since going near it ran the risk of me running into him. It was bad enough I'd have to see him at the Black Hat party tonight. Maybe it would be crowded enough I could avoid him or something. But that was stupid, because I couldn't avoid Hector forever, and I didn't want to either.

I paused beside a Pokémon display and pulled out my phone to text him, but couldn't find the right words. Nothing seemed appropriate for the situation. I wanted to ask if we were okay, but I was so worried the answer would be no. Or that he'd shut me down again like this morning.

God, I wished he had just told me what he wanted. One second he'd said the drawings meant something and that he'd wanted to kiss me for years, but then he'd said it was just sex and he didn't want anything from me. But if he didn't want to try a long distance relationship where did that leave us?

The problem was, I didn't know what I wanted either. Twenty-four hours ago I'd only seen Hector as a friend, but now my feelings for him were all jumbled and confused. There was no denying that our sexual chemistry was off the charts. Or that last night had been incredible. Or that I felt more comfortable with him than with anyone else in the world. But even if we didn't have the distance problem, I'd just gotten out of a serious relationship with Andy a week ago. I didn't want Hector to be a rebound, or to use him to make me feel better about my breakup or less alone. In the past, I'd jumped straight from one boyfriend to the next because I hated being single, but I was trying to change. Hector deserved better than that.

Of course, that was assuming he saw this as more than a one night stand. He'd never had a girlfriend in all the time I'd known him, but every now and then he had some brief hook-ups. Was that all he wanted—a short fling over the next few days? But then what?

Last night threatened to ruin everything between us, but I couldn't lose my friendship with him. He was not just the artist of my graphic novel, but the person I looked forward to talking to every day, the person I texted first with news, the person whose opinion I trusted the most about both my writing and my life. But it seemed the two of us were not meant to be anything more than friends.

And I wasn't sure if we could even be that now.

I gave up on texting Hector and went to that panel on writing and drawing diverse characters, even though I knew he might be there. Or because I *hoped* he would be there. But I scanned the room and didn't see him, and then spent the entire panel wishing he *was* there because I wanted to talk to him about it. I missed him so much already.

After the panel ended, I walked a couple blocks away to an area of the Gaslamp Quarter that wasn't quite as busy as around the convention center. I ducked into a bright, modern café and found the person I was looking for, already seated at a table.

Giselle Roberts.

I made my way over to her, completely star struck, still clueless as to why she wanted to talk to me. She was a curvy black woman in her forties with dark, wavy hair and confident eyes. She always looked stylish, and today she didn't disappoint in a form-fitting blue dress that was both sophisticated and sexy. Next to her I felt underdressed and sloppy in my ripped jeans and *Legend of Korra* t-shirt.

"Tara, right?" she asked, standing. She held out her hand. "I'm Giselle."

"So nice to meet you." I shook her hand and sat down, trying not to openly stare at her. The woman was a legend. Not only had she created some of my favorite TV shows, but she'd broken down barriers for women and people of color in entertainment and media, too. She was the closest thing I had to a role model.

"Thanks for having lunch with me," she said. "I know it's hard to find a spare moment during Comic-Con."

"No, thank *you*. I'm flattered you wanted to meet with me. And I'm sure you're even busier than I am."

She laughed, a sound that seemed to bubble out of her like champagne. "Luckily, I have assistants to do all the things I don't want to do."

"Oh. Of course." I wondered where her blond hipster assistant was. Off running an errand probably.

"I've been wanting to talk to you for a while." She leaned forward, pressing her hands flat on the table. "I love *Misfit Squad*. I've read it three times. I'm confident it's going to win a ton of awards next year."

My fingers tightened on the menu, the edges digging into my skin. I wasn't sure how to handle all this praise from someone I held in such high regard. "That's…wow. I'm honored. Thank you."

She waved a hand like it was nothing. "Just speaking the truth."

I let out a nervous laugh. "I'll have to make sure my editor gets you an early copy of the next book."

"Already taken care of." She leaned back in her chair and studied me. "I'm sure you're wondering why I asked you to meet me today. Part of the reason is that I wanted to sit down with you so I could fangirl over your book in person. And the other reason…" She took a long sip of water and I thought the suspense might kill me. "I'm starting my own superhero show and I want you to be a part of it."

"You…what?" Suddenly it seemed a lot harder to breathe in the café. Giselle Roberts doing a superhero show was the best news I'd heard all day at Comic-Con, and that was before it hit me that she wanted *me* to be a part of it.

"It's already getting a ton of interest from the networks. Think *Arrow* or *Heroes* but with a female lead. *Hunger Games* meets *Batman Begins*. It's going to be huge."

"I would watch that in an instant."

"Good. Because I want you to be one of the writers."

"Shut the front door." The words slipped out before I could stop them, but at least I'd used the censored version my mother would say. I couldn't imagine swearing in front of a classy woman like Giselle Roberts.

Luckily, she laughed, like she found my reaction amusing. "I already have the pilot done but I need good writers for the rest of the season. Based on your work on *Misfit Squad*, I know you'll be perfect."

"Wow." I sat back and let her words sink in. I couldn't believe she wanted me. I was just a small-time comic book writer whose graphic novel happened to get popular thanks to Hector's newfound fame. Working on a big TV show was way out of my league. Though I supposed writing for TV wouldn't be *that* different from writing comic books—I'd write the dialogue and action, then someone else would take it from there.

"I'm stunned. And flattered. And I think it sounds amazing. But I've never written for TV before."

"I'm sure you'll pick it up quickly. You'd have to move to Los Angeles immediately of course, but we'd cover all of your moving expenses."

I sucked in a breath, my head spinning with possibilities. Hector lived in Los Angeles. If I moved there maybe, just maybe, we could have a future together.

If he wanted that.

If *I* wanted that.

Or it would only make things more uncomfortable between us if our one night of passionate sex had been nothing more than that.

Or if it ruined our friendship forever.

Hang on, what was I thinking? I already had a job lined up. My *dream* job. The job I'd been working my ass off for years to get. They were also paying for my moving expenses to New York, and I'd already agreed on a start date in a few weeks. I couldn't back out now. But somehow this unbelievable job had practically fallen into my lap like some kind of *deus ex machina*, and how could I possibly say no to Giselle Freaking Roberts?

"Is something wrong?" she asked.

"No." I realized I'd been chewing on my fingernail and forced my hand down. "It's just that I've already accepted a job in New York at Ostrich Books in their comics division."

"How much are they offering?" she asked. "I'm sure I can beat it."

I swallowed hard. The job didn't pay much and New York was crazy expensive, but...I still wasn't sure. "Thank you, but it's not about the money, it's about the direction I want for my future career. Can I have some time to think it over? I'd love to work for you, but I have to be sure I'm making the best decision for me."

"I completely understand. I can give you a few days to think it over, but after that I'll have to look for someone else."

"I'll get back to you by the end of Comic-Con." It was Friday and Comic-Con ended on Sunday. That didn't give me much time, but I preferred it that way. It forced me to make a decision instead of waffling on it forever. And I had a feeling that once I talked to Hector he would help make the decision easier, one way or the other.

"That would be perfect. Let me give you my direct number." She handed me her card. "When you're ready to accept my offer, give me a call."

The food arrived, and as we ate she told me more about her show and asked me questions about *Misfit Squad*. It was hard to give coherent answers, because the entire time I kept thinking about how I had a job offer in Los Angeles, and what that could mean for me and Hector.

# CHAPTER TEN
## HECTOR

I've never been good at parties. Give me a beer and somewhere to sneak off to with my sketchbook and I was happy. But that wouldn't work at the Black Hat Comics party, not when Tara and I were the guests of honor.

The party was on an actual pirate ship docked in the marina and had a pirates vs. ninjas theme. The invite had said to pick a side and dress in costume, and upon arrival guests were handed either a pirate hat or a ninja hood. The Black Hat staff all had on wizard hats so they were neutral in the battle, while hired actors hung from ropes and engaged in sword fights in the shadows.

The most I could bother with was wearing all black—which I

would have done anyway—so they'd given me a ninja hood. Miguel had insisted I wear it, and I'd only agreed because I thought it would give me some anonymity in the crowd. But, no. Everyone wanted to talk to me—about the book, about the band, about *The Sound*. About Tara.

Where the hell was she? I was already on my third beer and there was no sign of her. I kept chugging them, hoping talking to people would get easier, but it never did. How did Jared do this shit? To think I'd actually gotten mad at him for hogging the interviews on *The Sound*. Now I'd give anything for him to be here to take some of the attention off me. But he was with Maddie and I was in the middle of a crowd of people who wanted to talk to me when all I could think about was Tara.

"When's the next book coming out?" someone asked, a question I'd heard about three hundred times already. I wanted to make a sign with the answer and hang it around my neck so I could point to it and grunt. Shit, I could do a whole FAQ, including other winners such as:

"Is there going to be a *Misfit Squad* movie?"

"When's your band's next album coming out?"

"What was it like being on *The Sound*?"

Over and over, the same annoying questions, nonstop. Even when I got a moment to myself the crowd of ninjas and pirates pressed around me, yapping away with their incessant small talk, making the warm summer air heavy and thick. I was sweaty and tired and just wanted to get the fuck out of there.

If I could escape before Tara arrived, even better.

Was she ditching the party on purpose to avoid me? If so, I didn't blame her. I'd been dreading the party for hours, knowing we'd have to face each other. Hell, I'd been a total asshole all day. Jared, Maddie, and Kyle had dragged me to a couple panels, but I barely remembered any of it. At least they'd known better than to ask me any questions. And I'd made sure to steer us clear of the diversity panel, knowing Tara would be there.

But I couldn't avoid her forever.

She walked onto the ship, her golden hair trailing from under a black pirate hat, and my chest tightened like a fist at the sight. Especially once the crowd parted enough for me to see her entire costume: a frilly, white, shoulder-less dress with a tight black corset over it that gave me an amazing view of her large breasts. It was so short it only just covered her curvy ass and left her shapely legs bare except for knee-high black boots. She looked so fucking hot I couldn't help but imagine bending her over the rail of the ship, pushing that skirt up, and taking her from behind.

Great, now I was hard as a rock and even more miserable.

She looked around like she wasn't sure she was in the right place, and then was swarmed by people. Somehow through the crowd she spotted me across the ship and our eyes met for a fraction of a second. I looked away quickly, unable to take any more of her gaze. If I had to actually talk to her I'd be really fucked.

I dove into the crowd in the opposite direction, debating whether I could avoid her for the rest of the night. How soon could I leave before it was rude? Maybe if I slipped out without Miguel noticing…

I was dragged into another conversation with two pirates about *The Sound* and suffered my way through it. Ten long minutes later, I saw Tara's pirate hat heading toward me, and I had to dart away again.

Hiding worked for another twenty minutes, until she found me at the front of the ship. She emerged from the crowd and backed me into the railing, with nothing but the ocean behind me. "There you are."

She looked determined, like a sexy pirate captain about to make me walk the plank. That corset was killing me with its tempting view of her chest. She had no idea how much I wanted to bury my face in her breasts. I chugged the last of my beer, my jeans growing uncomfortably tight again.

"Are you avoiding me?" she asked.

"No."

She frowned at me with those rosy lips. "Yes, you are."

I crushed the red cup in my hand and tossed it into the nearby trash can, turning away from her. But she wouldn't have any of that and grabbed my arm, pulling me back.

"Hector, please. Talk to me."

"What's there to say? Look, I'm sorry for this morning. I was a jerk. Let's just forget it, okay?"

Her fingers tightened around my bicep. She hadn't let go. "I don't want to forget it. I want to talk about it."

"There's nothing to talk about." The words were forced out through gritted teeth. "We live across the country from each other. After Comic-Con, things have to go back to the way they were before."

"What if they didn't?" She glanced around and lowered her voice. "I had my meeting with Giselle. She offered me a job as a writer on a new superhero TV show with a female lead. And the position is in LA."

"No shit?" I struggled to keep my face a blank canvas, but it was tough. That sounded like a pretty sweet gig, and she deserved it. And I didn't want to get too excited, but damn, the idea of her moving to LA was almost too good to be true. New paths opened up in my head like a sunrise dawning over a dark sky, and I was tempted to pull her into my arms and cover her face with kisses. For the first time ever I had real hope for a future with her.

But then reality crashed back in. She already had a job lined up. A job she'd been really excited about, that she'd worked her ass off to get, that she'd spent hours telling me about. She'd dreamed about working in publishing her entire life. How could she give that up?

She watched my reaction closely. "You don't seem as excited about this as I hoped you'd be."

"What about the job in New York?"

She turned to face the ocean, where the setting sun painted the sky in pink and purple. "I'm so torn. Both jobs are great opportunities. My heart was set on moving to New York and working in the comics division at Ostrich Books, but…"

I held my breath. "But what?"

"But this other job sounds like something I'd be stupid to turn down." She turned back to me, her eyes sparkling. "And you're in LA."

The words hit me so hard I stepped back. "Me?"

She closed the distance between us and placed a hand on my chest. "This morning you said you couldn't do long distance, and I get that, I do. But if I move to LA, you and I could try to be more than friends. That is, if you wanted to…"

Fuck yes I wanted to. Hearing that she wanted to try made something inside me ache in the best possible way. The selfish part of me wanted to get down on my knees and beg her to take the LA job so we could be together. I could already picture it: working with her on *Misfit Squad* in person instead of through email or chat; watching a movie with my arm around her, no longer thousand miles apart; being able to spend hours talking to her with no screen between us. And of course, all the hours I'd get to spend with her in bed. And against the wall. And in the shower…

But I'd be the biggest asshole in the world if I made her give up her dream for me. How could I live with myself if she chose the LA job to be near me and then hated it? Or what if things didn't work out between us? I didn't want her to resent me for the rest of her life because she'd followed me instead of her dream. Above all, I wanted her to be happy. Even if that meant it was without me.

"Please, Hector, say *something*," she said. "What do you think about all this?"

"I think..." I didn't know what to say, or how to express the thousands of conflicting feelings racing through me. Her hand was still on my chest and I pressed it against my heart, which I'm sure she could feel hammering away. "I don't want you to move to LA for me."

Her face crumpled. "Oh."

Shit, that wasn't the reaction I wanted. I was so bad at this. "Wait. Let me explain." With my free hand I cupped her chin and made her look up at me. "I want you to move to LA. More than anything. But I don't want to be the reason you pick one job or the other. I think you should choose the one you want the most, no matter where it is."

"I don't know which one I want the most."

"Take some time to think about it. When do you have to decide?"

"I have until Sunday. I hoped that talking to you would help me..."

"Sorry. You need to make this decision on your own."

She nodded, but still didn't look happy. I pulled her into my arms, wrapping her in a hug, burying my face in her silky hair.

She relaxed into my body with a long sigh, and I knew she needed this as much as I did, if not more.

"If you decide to move to New York, we'll still be friends," I said. "Everything will go back to the way it was before." That was such a lie. Nothing could ever be the same between us. But I wanted her to believe it anyway. "Whatever happens we'll be okay."

She peered up at me, her lips dangerously close to mine. "I don't want to lose you, Hector."

"You won't. I promise."

She lifted on her toes and kissed me, a soft, quick one, right on the border between friendly and more. I wasn't sure whether to return her kiss or not. I voted for not, only because if I kissed her I wouldn't be able to stop.

"What are we going to do for the rest of Comic-Con?" she asked, her hands still on my chest. "Today was horrible. I missed you so much."

"I missed you, too." Another repeat of today would kill me. I couldn't spend the next few days avoiding her, even if there was no hope for us beyond Sunday. If this was my one time to be with her in person I wanted to enjoy every second of it. "We have two more days together. We should have some fun, try to enjoy them."

"I like that idea. Just living in the moment. No worrying about the future or what will happen with us. And then when it's over...I guess we'll figure that out later."

"Exactly. What happens at Comic-Con stays at Comic-Con."

She laughed, and it was all worth it just to hear that sound. "I thought that only applied to Vegas."

We were interrupted by two artists in ninja costumes who wanted to introduce themselves. For a few minutes we talked shop, and I let Tara do most of the speaking while I admired the way she handled them. She was much better with people than I was.

Once they moved on, she said, "We should probably mingle."

"I don't want to mingle. I don't want to talk to anyone but you."

"Me either. We should leave before more people corner us."

"Miguel will be pissed."

"True. We'll have to sneak out."

"Good thing I have a ninja hood," I said, pulling it lower on my face with a grin.

She giggled. "Please, you're built like a tank. You'd be the worst ninja ever."

"Hey, I'm super stealthy! Besides, you're way too pretty to be a pirate."

She flashed me a coy smile. "You think I'm pretty?"

I took a piece of her golden hair in my fingers. "Girl, you know I think you're smoking hot. You're the sexiest pirate on this whole ship."

She gave a little shiver, even though it wasn't cold. "Let's get out of here."

# CHAPTER ELEVEN
## TARA

It took longer to sneak out of the party than we'd hoped, thanks to all the people who stopped us on our way off the ship. Thirty minutes later we were finally free, and together we headed back to the hotel we were both staying at courtesy of Black Hat Comics. Not a single person we passed gave me an odd look for walking around downtown San Diego in a skimpy pirate costume. One of the perks of Comic-Con.

Hector had taken off his ninja hood and donned his Villain Complex hat again. I was relieved things were back to normal between us (or as normal as they could be), although I wished he'd made my decision easier. I couldn't tell if he was truly happy about my job offer or not. I'd wanted him be thrilled that I might be moving near him, but he seemed especially closed off tonight. He was right though, I had to make that decision on my own, independent of my feelings for him.

But…how?

Even if I ignored my feelings for him the fact remained that in New York I wouldn't know anyone, whereas in LA I'd know Hector and his friends. If everything else was equal then having friends in a new city definitely edged one out over the other. But if this thing with Hector ended badly, I'd wind up alone in LA, too.

I had to make my decision without factoring him in…somehow.

"Tell me about LA," I said, as we walked along the brightly lit streets packed with people in cosplay and pedicabs decorated with advertising. "I've never been. What's it like?"

"Um, I've lived there my whole life, so I'm not sure how to compare it to anywhere else. It's crazy expensive to live there. It's big and spread out. There's a shitload of traffic and public transportation sucks. The weather is great year-round, but you'll probably miss having a real winter with snow and stuff."

So far he wasn't making it sound too appealing, almost like he *wanted* me to choose New York. "Cold weather is fun for the first month or two, then it gets old pretty fast. What else?"

"There's a million things to do there. Shopping, clubs, beaches, hiking, restaurants of every type of cuisine you can think of...." He rubbed the back of his neck. "Shit, I don't know. I'm starting to sound like a tour guide or something."

"Okay, then tell me something *you* love about LA."

"Hmm. I like the music scene, obviously. Love the art museums. I've spent many hours wandering through LACMA and the Getty."

I smiled at the image of big, brooding Hector spending all day in an art museum. It was one of my favorite things about him—he was this perfect image of hulking masculinity, yet completely owned the fact that he was an artist, too.

We turned onto a quieter street before he spoke again. "But I guess my favorite thing is the diversity. Anyone can find a place to belong there. Queer, straight, brown, white, vegan, goth, hipster, whatever—it's all good. No one bats an eyelash at me being in a band with two white boys. Or when my cousin Carlos married another guy, no one freaked out. Well, except my *abuelita*, but she's old fashioned to the extreme. And even she got over it pretty fast."

A place to belong. The one thing I'd been searching for my entire life. "That sounds nice. And so different from where I grew up."

"Your parents would probably freak out if you brought home a Mexican guy, eh?"

Was he implying that he wanted to meet my parents? I tried to study his face, but it was hard to read his expression in the dark. "Maybe, but I'm used to their disapproval."

I'd grown up in a huge, conservative Midwestern family complete with stay-at-home mom, white picket fence, and Golden Retriever. It sounded idyllic, but as I'd mentioned at the *Misfit Squad* panel, I'd always been an outcast. My small town in Nebraska had been suffocating and I'd escaped the first chance I could.

It was only once I started college in Boston that my eyes opened to a bigger world with all sorts of different people in it. I discovered just how sheltered I'd been my entire life, and that I wasn't fundamentally flawed or inherently strange for being different. Now I felt like a stranger every time I returned home.

My family loved me, of course, but they'd always thought I was crazy for reading books instead of watching football, for staying in to write stories instead of going to parties, or for wanting more from my life than following in my mother's footsteps and popping out babies as soon as I could. I didn't think a single one of them had read *Misfit Squad* yet, though they'd all said how proud they were of me. And it was true, they wouldn't love the idea of me dating a Mexican guy either.

Good thing I didn't care what they thought.

"What about your grandmother?" I asked. "Would she be upset if you brought home a white girl?"

"Nah. I'm sure she'd love it if I married some super traditional Mexican girl who spoke perfect Spanish and could make tortillas from scratch, but that's not going to happen. In the end, she just wants me to be happy."

I tried not to read too much into his words, but I so wanted to be the girl who made him happy. How had that happened? Yesterday, I'd only seen him as a friend, and now I wanted him to take me home to meet his family. It scared me a little, how quickly my feelings had changed for him and how fast this was progressing. We were almost, but not quite, talking about a future together. Feeling things out without making any actual plans or firm commitments to each other. Skirting the line into dangerous territory but not yet crossing over it.

Time to bring the conversation back to safer waters. "Will she and your sisters be okay with you gone for the next month?"

"They'll be fine. Rosalia just turned sixteen so she's old enough to help look after Yasmine and Ana now. I hate to leave them for that long but this tour is important, and we're getting some good money for it. Enough that I'll be able to send a bunch home to my parents, too."

"Have you spoken to your parents recently?" I asked softly, knowing it was a difficult subject for him.

"Last week, after the show ended. They were able to watch it while it was on TV, which was cool." He sighed. "I wanted to visit them this summer but the timing didn't work out. Maybe after the tour. I haven't seen them in forever."

Hector's parents had been deported to Mexico when he was thirteen. He and his three little sisters had all moved in with his grandmother, and he still lived with them so he could help out with the bills and taking care of them. He rarely talked about it—or about anything involving his past—but I knew it was a heavy burden on him sometimes. And that he missed his parents like crazy.

"I wish I could help them out more," he continued. "Find a way to get them back here."

I took his hand in mine, wishing I could help *him* in some way. "You do everything you can, and more."

"I hate that they haven't been around for most of my sisters' lives. Rosalia's driving now, Yasmine just got her first boyfriend, and Ana started wearing makeup. Shit, they're all growing up way too fast if you ask me, and our parents are *missing* it."

He sounded so pained, it made my heart ache for him. "Maybe with the money from your new recording deal you'll be able to visit them more."

"Yeah, maybe."

I squeezed his hand and made my voice light, trying to brighten the mood. "I've heard so much about your sisters. I'd love to meet them sometime."

His shoulders relaxed and he returned the squeeze. "They wanted to come to Comic-Con so bad. Especially Yasmine. She's obsessed with that *Arrow* show and told me to get the guy's autograph."

"That guy *is* pretty hot. He's always running around half-naked on the show, like they have some shirtless quota to fill every episode. Not that I'm complaining. I mean, those abs, my god."

"You trying to make me jealous? Maybe I should take my shirt off so you won't think about that other guy."

I laughed, relieved he was joking around again. "I wouldn't complain if you did. You have incredible abs, too."

"Oh yeah?" He quickly tugged his black shirt over his head. "Done."

He shouldn't be allowed to remove his shirt like that without some kind of warning first. I shoved him lightly in the side, mainly so I could touch him. "Show off."

He grinned and flexed his arms in an exaggerated way, and it was hard not to stare at his rippling muscles. "Sorry, should I put my shirt back on?"

"No, definitely not. In fact, you should never wear a shirt again. You'd be doing the world a favor."

He let out a deep, hearty laugh that rumbled down my spine, and it made my day knowing I'd caused it. I made a resolution to try to make him laugh more often.

Ahead of us, a girl yelled, "Oh my god!" She dragged her friend down the sidewalk, and they were both dressed in identical Slave Leia costumes from *Return Of The Jedi*. "You're Hector, from Villain Complex!"

Hector didn't move to put his shirt back on, but he shifted on his feet, like he wanted to bolt. "Hey…"

"Your band is so freaking hot," Slave Leia No. 2 said, leaning forward and drawing attention to her barely there gold top and impressive cleavage. "I watched every episode of *The Sound*."

"Me, too," the first one said. She played with her long braid, her eyes glued to Hector's naked chest. "I love you guys."

"Um, thanks," he said.

"Aren't you two cold in those costumes?" I asked, eyeing their exposed legs. I wasn't wearing much more than them, but I wanted to make it clear that I was with Hector.

They cast me a confused glance, like they wondered what I was doing there. The first Slave Leia took a step closer to Hector, invading his personal space. "Hey, you want to come party with us?"

The second girl moved in too, licking her lips. "It'll be fun, we promise."

I didn't have a violent bone in my body, yet I had the sudden, primal urge to growl and shove them back, to make sure they knew he was mine. My god, what had gotten into me?

"Sorry, I'm busy tonight." Hector placed a hand on the small of my back, an intimate gesture not lost on them…or on me.

"She can come along, if you want," Slave Leia  No. 2 said, with another brief glance my way.

I laughed. "Yeah, that's going to happen, oh…how about *never*."

Hector tried to suppress a grin. "Thanks for the offer, but we're good."

We walked away, his hand a steady, almost possessive presence on my lower back. I leaned against his side and the heat rising off his skin enveloped me.

Sorry ladies, Hector was all mine. At least for the next few days.

I nudged him with my hip. "You better put your shirt back on. I don't want any other girls getting ideas."

"That was unusual. They always go for Jared, or sometimes Kyle. Never me." He removed his Villain Complex hat and shoved it into his jeans, shaking his hair out. "Not sure I like the attention."

"No? I thought every guy dreamed of scantily clad women inviting him for a threesome."

He pinned me with his smoldering dark eyes. "Not this guy."

The intensity of his gaze took my breath away. The chemistry between us was thick, the desire so strong I could practically smell it in the air. He was still shirtless, a large, handsome, solid mountain of a man. A mountain I wanted to climb and conquer.

We entered the hotel and his hand slipped lower, to the top of my butt, pressing into the thin fabric of my dress. As we stepped into the elevator my eyes trailed from his hips up his defined chest to his strong jaw shadowed by dark stubble. I had the strongest urge to press my lips to it, to feel that roughness against my mouth. He had to know what he was doing to me standing there in nothing but his jeans.

He didn't hit the button for his floor, and I didn't comment on it. My breath quickened at the thought of him coming to my room. I wasn't sure what we were doing, but didn't want to stop. Inviting him inside would only complicate things further between us. The more time I spent with him, the more I never wanted to let him go, and the harder my decision got.

Once at my room, he leaned against the door, the sexual masculinity practically rolling off him. "Are you camping with us tonight in the Hall H line?"

I reached up to wrap my finger around one of his short curls, unable to help myself. "I don't know…"

"Come on, it'll be fun. We have food, alcohol, and Cards Against Humanity. What more could you want?"

I laughed. "A warm bed?"

"I'll keep you warm. Although I have to warn you, I only have one sleeping bag…"

Well, that settled it. The thought of sleeping against Hector under the stars was too good to pass up. "Okay. Just give me a minute to change my clothes."

"Are you sure?" His eyes roved up and down my body in a way that sent a rush of warmth between my thighs. "Cause I could look at you in that costume all night long."

The chemistry between us threatened to combust at any moment. Screw it, we'd both agreed to have fun for the rest of Comic-Con—and I had a great idea how to start.

"I could keep it on a little longer." I slipped my fingers into the belt loops of his jeans and pulled him closer. "Do you want to come inside?"

# CHAPTER TWELVE
## HECTOR

As soon as the door shut, we were on each other. My discarded shirt hit the floor while our bodies and mouths joined in a desperate, hungry crush. Tara's hands were instantly on my chest, stroking me all over like she couldn't get enough of my skin. I knew exactly how she felt.

I pressed rough kisses down her delicate neck to her bare shoulder to the top of her lush, soft breasts. They'd been shoved up and forced together thanks to her tight corset, nearly exposing her nipples. I sucked on them through the fabric, scraping at them with my teeth, making her whimper.

She tangled her fingers in my hair and yanked me back to her lips. Any worries about what we were doing vanished as she slipped her tongue into my mouth. Our future together was uncertain, but none of that mattered when she kissed me like that.

"Ever since you took your shirt off, I've been dying to do this," she said, licking across my jaw and down my neck, sending hot sparks throughout my entire body.

"Your costume has been driving me crazy all night," I said, though it came out more like a growl. "That corset. That short dress. Those boots. I've been walking around hard for the past hour."

"Have you?" She slipped a hand between us to check the front of my jeans and I groaned as she rubbed me there.

"Damn, girl. I wanted to go slower this time, but you're making that difficult."

"I don't want slow. Or gentle. Not tonight."

"Thank god."

I gripped her ass and yanked her against me, grinding her hips against mine. She kissed me with the same ferocity while I slid a hand down her thigh, forcing up the bottom of her dress, finding the edge of her panties. I tore at them, pushing them aside, and she moaned against my mouth as I made contact. Fuck, she was already so warm and slick and ready for me, and I had barely even touched her.

I fondled her breast with one hand, teasing her nipple through the corset, while my other hand continued exploring between her thighs. I shoved her legs apart with my knee, making her open wider for me. She clutched my arms and made the most delicious sounds as I slipped my fingers into her, one by one. Her nails scraped against my skin while I stroked her both inside and out and the slight pain made me even harder. Soon she was holding on to me for dear life, eyes closed, her face even more beautiful as she came undone. It gave me so much satisfaction knowing I had the power to do that.

Before she could recover, I turned her around, pushing her toward the edge of the bed. "All night I've thought about taking you from behind in that costume. And now I'm going to do exactly that."

"Oh god, yes," she said, arching against me.

I nudged her forward and she crawled onto the bed on her hands and knees, still wearing those knee-high black boots that made her legs look sexy as hell. I shoved her dress up around her hips, taking in her perfect, round ass and every other inch of exposed skin.

"God, you are so hot." I bent my head to taste between her thighs, giving her one long, lazy lick to let her know how much I meant it. She rewarded me with another of those sexy moans, and I couldn't wait to be inside her. I quickly undid my jeans, too eager to take them off completely, though I managed to grab a condom from my pocket and get that on.

Still standing, I palmed her smooth legs, so pale against my own skin, and spread her wider. She completely opened for me and glanced over her shoulder with raw lust in her eyes, turning me on even more.

I found her entrance and pushed just the tip inside to tease her, but she moaned and pressed back against me, trying to take me deeper. Fuck, that was hot. She really didn't want gentle or slow, my sexy little wench. But I was in control here, not her. I grasped her hips, holding her in place, and rubbed up and down, in and out, just enough to make her beg.

And oh, did she beg.

"Please, Hector. *Please.*"

I'd never heard anything sweeter in my life. How could I refuse when she asked like that?

With my hands on her hips, I plunged inside her in one smooth motion, all the way to the hilt. She gasped and threw her head back, her golden hair falling around her bare shoulders. Her pirate hat must have fallen off at some point in our frenzy.

At this angle I filled her completely and oh god it felt so good, so fucking tight. I wanted to take my time, but each thrust nearly sent me over the edge. Especially when she pressed back against my body with the same urgency. There was no holding back or going slow, and there was definitely no way I could be gentle. There was just this primal need for each other, like we were animals. Tonight she was mine, and I was hers, no matter what happened after this weekend.

My fingers dug into her skin as I pumped in and out with wild abandon, unable to control myself. She worked with me, rocking back and forth in time with my movements, forcing me deeper and deeper. Her hands clawed at the sheets, fisting them as she cried out. It was too much, and I was already so close, but I needed to take her along with me.

With one hand curled around her waist, I reached between her legs, rubbing her in exactly the right spot to make her shudder. It wasn't long before the orgasm hit her hard and she pushed back against me, clenching around me, shouting my name into the air. I rode through it, never letting up my pace, not wanting this moment to ever end. But I couldn't hold on and soon gave myself completely to her, the pleasure so intense I thought I might black out.

I slipped out of her and collapsed onto the bed, pulling her on top of me. She draped her arms around my neck and kissed me softly, her body relaxing into mine. We were both still partly dressed, our clothes a messy tangle around us, but neither of us moved to fix them. Soon our breath and heartbeats slowed together in sync.

"Last night was incredible," she said. "But that? That might have topped it."

I chuckled and tightened my arms around her. "You're good for my ego."

"I'm only speaking the truth."

One of her hands smoothed up and down my chest, tracing every ridge and curve with her fingers like she was fascinated by them. "I could touch you for hours."

"I wouldn't complain." I closed my eyes as she continued her investigation of my body. All my hours at the gym were definitely paying off. I didn't work out to impress women, but to keep my stamina up for shows and because it helped me stay calm and grounded. Tara's appreciation was just a huge bonus.

She propped herself up on one arm to look at me. "What does *te quiero* mean?"

I tensed and nearly jumped off the bed. "What?"

"You said it at the end, over and over."

Jesus, I'd said that out loud? I'd never done that before. I only spoke Spanish with my *abuelita*, since my sisters and I grew up speaking English to each other. But that moment at the end with Tara had been so intense it must have slipped out.

"It means, 'I want you.'" I gave her the literal translation instead of the one I'd really meant: I love you. At least I hadn't said *te amo*. She'd probably be able to guess the meaning of that one.

She smiled, idly running her fingers through my hair. "I like it when you speak Spanish. Even if I have no idea what you're saying."

"Oh yeah?" I switched to Spanish, whispering in her ear. "Tara, you are my sunshine, my moonlight, the light of my life. I love you, no matter what happens this weekend." Even though it was cheesy as hell it felt good to confess that, and no one would ever know what I'd said except me.

"Mmm." She nuzzled her face into my neck. "What did you say?"

"That you look so damn sexy I want to take you all over again." I'd never before been so happy that she'd taken French as her language elective in college. I kissed her forehead. "But we need to get going."

"Too bad."

"Later. We still have another night before Comic-Con ends." And after that…

I forced myself not to think about it. All that mattered was right now, this moment together, and it was enough. We'd work the rest out later.

# CHAPTER THIRTEEN
# TARA

Hector's band was already in the lobby by the time we got down there, along with Alexis and two of Maddie's friends—Carla, a tall, stunningly beautiful black girl with wild curls and a *MythBusters* t-shirt, and Julie, an Asian girl dressed in a steampunk Wonder Woman costume. Maddie and Jared were cosplaying as Princess Leia and Han Solo, and they were insanely cute together. Maybe I should have worn my pirate costume after all—but it needed a good wash after what had just been done in it.

Jared explained that we had to hit the store to get food and drinks before joining the Hall H line. We all stepped outside the hotel as one big cluster, carrying backpacks with clothes, sleeping bags, and games. It felt good to be surrounded by friends again, even if I didn't know them very well. If I moved to LA I'd be hanging out with these people a lot, I hoped. Tonight would be a tiny glimpse of what my life might be like if I chose the LA job…and Hector.

"Where's your Villain Complex hat?" Jared asked.

Hector ran a hand through his short curls and scowled. "I stopped wearing it because people kept recognizing me from the show. It got annoying."

"What? No one's recognized me so far. Maybe I should wear the hat from now on."

"It wouldn't go with your costume," I said.

"True." Jared grinned, looking back and forth between me and Hector. "Glad to see you two patched it up. I thought I'd have to hug it out of him."

"Keep your arms to yourself," Hector growled.

"You know you want some of this." Jared grabbed him in a big hug and tried to kiss him, while Hector squirmed away.

"Knock it off," Hector said, but I could tell he secretly loved it. The two of them started wrestling and then Jared darted down the street with Hector chasing after him, both of them laughing. They reminded me of my brothers, who constantly beating each other up with smiles on their faces.

"Are they always like this?" I asked Maddie, moving to walk at her side.

"Pretty much. Sometimes Kyle joins in, too." She watched them with obvious affection. "I'm so glad you could make it tonight. Camping out for Hall H is a Comic-Con tradition everyone has to do at least once."

"How could I resist the lure of sleeping in front of a convention center with thousands of other sweaty, tired nerds?"

"Exactly! And now we can discuss your costume for the Masquerade. Julie's already putting it together."

"Oh, cool. What Batman villain am I going to be?"

Julie explained her plans for my costume, and I got even more excited. She eyed me up and down. "We have some clothes that might work, but it would help if I knew what you brought to Comic-Con."

"I don't have much. Just a couple t-shirts, some jeans, and a pirate costume." I described the costume for her and her face lit up.

"Yes! I think I can make that work for what I have in mind. We'll have to get a bowtie and a top hat, but I'm sure someone is selling those here."

"If it's too much trouble don't worry about it. I don't need a costume."

"No way. Challenge accepted!"

"Trust me, she lives for this stuff," Maddie said.

"I love your costume," I said, gesturing at Julie's steampunk Wonder Woman outfit. "It's so badass and clever at the same time. Did you make it, too?"

"I did! Thanks!" She donned her goggles and tossed her long, black hair over her shoulder, exuding major confidence and sexuality. I liked her instantly.

Carla shook her head, smiling. "Don't encourage her."

Julie struck another pose, hands on her hips. "You're just upset that guys are looking at me instead of you for once."

"That must be it."

As we walked, we discussed my costume in more detail and made arrangements for us to get together a few hours before the Masquerade. Alexis joined us and added her own thoughts, and I felt this overwhelming sense of belonging and happiness bubble up inside me. Hector's friends had immediately accepted me as one of their group and involved me in all their plans. They really felt like *my* people.

Hector moved to my side, sliding a hand around my waist. "Are these pretty ladies bothering you, Tara?"

"We totally are," Julie said, grinning at me. "You should rescue her."

Hector rolled his eyes, but the other girls giggled and gave us some space.

"Everything okay?" he asked.

I couldn't contain the smile bursting out of me. "Everything is great. I really like your friends."

He chuckled and kissed me on the forehead. "Yeah, they're not so bad."

We entered the supermarket, and Hector and the others

stopped inside the entrance next to a row of cupcakes with tiny superheroes on them. Jared rubbed his hands together. "Time to play a little game."

"Ooh, I've been dying to play this ever since Maddie told me about it," Julie said.

Alexis groaned. "Don't tell me you guys still play Supermarket Treasure Hunt."

"What's that?" I asked.

"A game they invented when we were teenagers," she said. "I assumed they'd outgrow it but I guess not."

Kyle draped an arm around her. "If I recall, *you* were the one who invented the game."

She laughed and gave him a quick kiss. "That is *so* not how I remember it."

We all crowded around Jared, who seemed to be the unspoken leader of the group. "Since there are so many of us we're going to do a team version of Supermarket Treasure Hunt. Grab a partner and a shopping cart and find the three craziest, weirdest, and, most importantly, the funniest items you can find. Make sure they all follow a theme for bonus points. Since this is Comic-Con, I expect some seriously messed up shit. Meet at the banana stand in ten minutes and we'll vote on the winner. Now...go!"

The others ran off, grabbing carts while hooting and cheering. Hector grasped my hand and tugged me toward the alcohol aisle. "Come on. I saw some weird shit in this section when I picked up beer yesterday."

I laughed and followed him, snagging a cart along the way. I'd never done anything like this before, but I could already imagine what my life would be like if I moved to LA...and I liked the image. Especially if it included more of Hector holding my hand.

In the alcohol aisle, we scanned the options quickly and pointed out a few things that might work. Then I spotted cans of alcoholic whip cream. In multiple flavors. "Look at this!"

"Perfect."

"We need one of each." I grabbed them off the shelf and dumped them into our cart.

"You're a natural at this game." He pulled me against his chest and kissed me deeply, like I was the only thing in his entire world. And for a minute, he was the only thing in mine.

Once we finally broke apart I checked the time. "We need to hurry. I'll look through the other aisle, you keep working on this one."

He nodded and I took off. I scoured the wine section in the next aisle, trying to move fast with the clock ticking away. I was about to grab a bottle that said Dry Sack Wine (ha!) when a familiar voice behind me said, "Tara?"

Oh no.

Andy.

"Hey." I spun around, feeling guilty even though I had no reason to be. Thank god he hadn't caught me a minute ago when

I'd had my tongue inside Hector's mouth. Not that I'd done anything wrong by kissing Hector, but it would have made this moment that much more uncomfortable. "What are you doing here?"

He wore a black polo shirt with a tiny Rubik's Cube for the logo, and his dark blond hair was messier than normal, hanging nearly into his hazel eyes. He was ridiculously handsome, and my stomach tightened at the sight—a reminder that I still cared about him.

"Grabbing some beer." He walked over to me, frowning. "I texted you like five times. I thought we were going to have dinner tonight."

"You did?" Shit, shit, shit. I'd completely forgotten I'd told Andy I would text him when the party was over. "I'm so sorry! My phone was on silent and the party ran late and..."

I cringed inwardly at the white lie, but I couldn't exactly say I'd forgotten to call him because Hector had been banging my brains out. I fumbled through my bag for my phone and yep, there they were: five texts from Andy, plus a voicemail. I hadn't checked it while Hector had been distracting me so thoroughly, but now I felt like a total bitch.

"That's okay. We can go get something to eat now." It was such an Andy response. He was always polite, always kind, always forgiving.

"Oh, um...I can't." Ugh, I really was the worst.

Hector turned onto the aisle with our cart, but froze midstride when he saw Andy. The two of them stared at each other for the longest minute of my life. My perfect night instantly turned into my worst nightmare.

Andy slowly looked back and forth between me and Hector. "Ah. I didn't realize the two of you were hanging out tonight." He held out his hand. "I'm Andy. Tara's told me so much about you."

Hector shook his hand, though he looked like he'd rather touch a dead fish, despite being allergic to them. "Hey, man. Nice to meet you."

I caught myself biting my nails again and forced myself to stop. "We, uh, ran into each other at the Black Hat party, and um..."

"Cool, cool," Andy said, shoving his hands in his pockets.

An awkward silence settled over us and I had no idea how to end it. Finally, Hector cleared his throat. "I'm going to find the others. See you later, Andy."

After he left the tension eased by a small percent and I stepped closer to Andy. "I'm really sorry about dinner. Maybe we can do something tomorrow? I'm busy in the morning, and I have a signing in the afternoon, and then I'll be at the Masquerade that night, but..."

"I'll definitely be at your signing. Maybe we can grab a coffee after?"

"That'd be great."

Another uncomfortable silence. My ten minutes for the game

were probably up by now. I glanced behind me, trying to figure out a polite way of ending this conversation. "Well, I better go…"

"Oh. Yeah. Me, too."

Andy looked so lost and alone I almost invited him to join us tonight, but that wasn't my place. Instead, I hugged him and was surprised by how comforting his familiar, easy presence was. "It was good to see you."

"You too." His hands tangled in my hair as he squeezed me back. "I missed you."

"I missed you, too."

It was true…except now that I'd been with Hector my time with Andy seemed shallow and lacking in comparison. If I was completely honest with myself, one of the reasons it had never worked with Andy (or any of the previous guys) was because Hector had always been there. He'd been unattainable, but even so there had been an ever-present feeling of wrongness with anyone else. I'd felt guilty, almost like I'd been cheating on both guys. I'd done nothing wrong, but it had always *felt* wrong.

I still cared for Andy a lot. How could I not, when we'd been together a year? He'd been a good boyfriend that entire time. There had never been anything *wrong* with him. He was a great guy, but it was clear now—I'd never been able to love Andy the way he deserved because there had always been the shadow of another man in my thoughts.

I left him in the wine aisle and found the others waiting for me by the bananas. They gave me curious looks as I approached, but didn't ask where I'd been. Hector searched my eyes and I gave him a weak smile.

"Sorry," I said to the group. "I ran into a friend."

"No problem," Jared said. "Now that you're here, we can present our goods. Maddie is our defending champion, so our team will go first."

"Our theme is, 'who thought this was a good idea?'" Maddie reached into a basket and pulled out her finds. "We have cappuccino potato chips. Watermelon Oreos. And…bacon mac and cheese ice cream! All of which somehow got past many committees to arrive on our shelves."

"I can't decide if I'm intrigued or horrified," Kyle said.

"Same," Julie said. "We should buy each of them and try them tonight."

"Good idea," Jared said. "Okay, Kyle and Alexis, you're next."

"The theme for tonight is 'naughty food.'" Alexis said, while Kyle displayed the items one by one. "We start with some delicious Perky Jerky, then move on to Breast Munchies. And for a happy ending, some creamy white finishing sauce."

"Gross," Carla said, wrinkling her nose.

"We could not even make this stuff up," Kyle said, shaking his head.

"Yeah, not super tempted by any of those," Jared said. "Okay, who's next?"

"We'll go," Julie said. She gestured to Carla, who looked

embarrassed as she pulled out the items in their cart. "Behold, three items we call, 'so wrong, it's right.' First up, condoms with superheroes on them. I think some of you might need to buy these." That got a few grins from the group. "But for those of us flying solo this weekend, we can still have some fun with a *Harry Potter* vibrating wand."

"What the actual fuck," Hector said.

Alexis covered her eyes. "No! My childhood!"

"Okay, then maybe I can tempt you with this perfectly shaped frosting decorator?" Julie waved at the item in Carla's hand that looked suspiciously like a clear plastic dildo.

Maddie shook her head. "That is definitely wrong, but I'm not sure it ever goes all the way into right."

Julie grinned. "True, it's a bit small for my tastes."

Everyone laughed and some of my apprehension over seeing Andy faded away. This felt good and right, and I couldn't spend my entire time at Comic-Con worrying about him. I had to find my own happiness, and he had to find his.

"Very nice," Jared said, once the laughter died out. "And now, our final team…"

Hector raises his eyebrows at me, and I nodded for him to continue. He grabbed a six pack that he must have picked up while I was talking to Andy. "We call this theme, 'you sure you want to drink that?' First, we have sticky toffee pudding ale." He triumphantly held up another six pack. "Along with…spicy chipotle beer."

The group all groaned or made faces, and Julie said, "I'm going to throw up."

"It's either going to be amazing or disgusting," Maddie said.

"I'm voting for disgusting," Kyle said.

"Let's buy it and find out," Jared said. "What's your third item?"

Hector grinned and pulled out two cans of the item I'd picked out. "For the grand finale: alcoholic whip cream in a wide variety of flavors."

"Okay, we definitely have to get those," Julie said. "All the flavors. Multiple cans."

"Don't worry, we're buying some," I said.

"Thank you, Hector and Tara," Jared said. "All right. Time to pick a winner. Keep in mind you're not allowed to vote for your own team."

He went through all the teams and we each voted for our favorite, but it was clear that Carla and Julie were the winners. For their prize they got bragging rights for the rest of the night, which Julie seemed much more excited about than Carla.

We all split up again to put the items back and get food and drinks for our little evening picnic. I didn't see Andy again, luckily.

Now if only I could scrub the lingering guilt and sadness from my mind, I could get back to having a good time.

# CHAPTER FOURTEEN
## HECTOR

The line for Hall H was already long by the time we got there. It wove back and forth on the grass outside the convention center, where a cold breeze came in off the nearby marina. Our group got a spot in line and spread out our sleeping bags, settling in for the night.

I popped open one of the sticky toffee pudding ales and took a whiff. "Well, it smells good." I held it out for Tara, who took it and nodded. "Anyone else brave enough to try?"

A few of the others agreed, and I passed the bottles around. I grabbed one for myself, popping the lid off with my bottle opener keychain.

"Okay, we down it on the count of three. One…two…three!" We all took sips, and I nearly gagged. "Fuck, that is repulsive."

Jared made a choking sound. "It's like if a cat pissed on an ice cream cone."

"If someone made a cake, waited 'til it got moldy and then ate it, that's what this would taste like," Tara said.

"It can't be *that* bad," Maddie said.

"Oh no, it really is. Try it." Tara handed the beer to her.

She took a sip and made a face. "Okay, you were right. It is that bad."

The spicy chipotle beer wasn't quite as terrible, but not something I'd ever buy again either. We tore open the rest of our food and snacks, trying out the items we'd found in the store and testing the different flavors of alcoholic whip cream on each one.

"I have a great idea for what to use these for," Jared said, spraying some of the whip cream in his mouth. He pulled Maddie in for a kiss and she licked it off his mouth.

"Later," she said.

I threw a bag of chips at them. "Knock it off, you two."

Jared grinned. "Don't tell me you didn't have the exact same idea."

He'd got me there. My eyes darted to Tara, who smiled at me but then looked down at the grass. She'd seemed quiet and reserved ever since we'd run into Andy.

That moment had been pretty fucking weird for me, too. I'd spent the last year resenting Andy for being with the girl I loved, even though he seemed like a decent enough guy and he'd always treated Tara well. If I had to pick some other guy to date her I doubt I'd find anyone better than him. In a different situation, he and I might even be friends. But from the way he'd looked at Tara in the supermarket I'd known he wasn't over her, and something had definitely changed in her after seeing him, too.

Did she still have feelings for him? The two of them had just broken up, and I sure as hell didn't want to be a rebound. I knew how Tara worked—she immediately moved from one boyfriend to the next, and I was the newest link in her chain. But I didn't want to be a temporary boyfriend. If we did this I wanted to be the last guy she was with. The one she stayed with forever.

We spent the next few hours eating, drinking, and playing Cards Against Humanity, and Tara relaxed with each round. It was past midnight by the time we climbed into our sleeping bags to get a few hours of rest before they let us inside Hall H early in the morning.

Like I'd warned Tara earlier, I only had one sleeping bag, but it was a two-person bag because I could barely fit in a normal-sized one on my own. Tara and I both slipped inside, but she didn't snuggle up against me as I'd hoped. Instead we lay on our sides, facing each other but not touching.

"You okay?" I asked, keeping my voice low since the others were trying to sleep.

"Yeah." She sighed. "Running into Andy just threw off my night, I guess."

"Trust me, it wasn't my favorite thing either."

"No, I suppose not." She rolled onto her back, staring up at the stars.

"You two were pretty serious. Makes sense you'd be upset after running into him."

"It's extra hard because we broke up only a few days ago." She let out a sad little laugh. "And yeah, we were pretty serious. My parents loved him, too. Wanted us to get married and have babies the second we graduated college."

The thought of her marrying Andy and having blond babies with him made me want to punch something. Or someone. Or myself. I wasn't sure.

And of course her parents loved him. From what she'd told me, they'd rather have their daughter end up as Tara Smith—or whatever Andy's last name was—than Tara Fernandez.

"Is that what you wanted?" I asked.

"No. I'm not ready for any of that. I think Andy was, though. And sometimes the fantasy did sound pretty good...." She covered her face with her hands. "God, I'm such a mess. I'm sorry."

I didn't need to punch myself after all, 'cause her words hit me right in the gut. There was a whole future she'd imagined with Andy that had never included me. She obviously still had feelings for him, even if she didn't want to admit it. We were having fun this weekend but it didn't even come close to what they'd had. And how could it? They'd been together a year. We'd been friends for three, but she'd never thought about me as anything more than that until what? Yesterday?

"Enough about me." She propped herself up on an elbow to face me. "Tell me something about you I don't know."

"Um, there's not much you don't know after all this time."

"No? You never talk about your past. I want to know everything!"

I hated talking about my past. Or thinking about it at all, if I could help it. But her enthusiasm made me grin, and for once I didn't mind. "Like what?"

She played with the chain around her neck. "Like…how did you become friends with Jared and Kyle? I know you met in high school, but I want the whole story of how the band got started."

"Not that exciting of a story, but okay. I was always pretty good at drawing and shit, and my *abuelita* got me a scholarship at this fancy high school for visual and performing arts. Freshman year, Jared and I got teamed up for a project in English class where we had to write a poem and create a corresponding art piece to go with it. He wrote the words, I drew something, and after that we started hanging out."

"Sounds kind of like what we do for *Misfit Squad*." She rested her hand on my chest, tracing idle patterns in my shirt. "Did you like going to school there?"

"For the most part. It was a good school, but there were some guys who liked to give me shit for being the poor scholarship kid. First time Jared punched one of them, I knew he would always have my back."

Her eyebrows shot up. "The *first* time?"

"Uh." I coughed. "We used to get in a lot of fights, but that was years ago. We're both done with that shit now."

"Good." Her hand moved up to my neck, her fingers warm against my skin. The more I talked the more she touched me. I'd have to remember that. "Then what?"

"I used to hang out at Jared and Kyle's house all the time. One day I tried out their drum kit and was hooked. Jared said we should start a band and it took off from there." I shrugged. "Like I said, not that exciting of a story. Though it's kind of crazy how fast it all went down. Seems like only yesterday we were playing frat parties and parking lot shows, not huge stadiums."

"It wasn't *that* fast. You worked hard for years to get the band to where it is now. You practiced every night for hours and hours. I remember, even if you don't."

"That's true." I brushed a strand of golden hair away from her face. "Any more questions?"

She searched my eyes, opening and closing her mouth like she wanted to ask something but was hesitant. How bad could it be? I draped an arm around her waist. "You can ask me anything."

"Why have you been single all these years, Hector?"

I released her, my whole body tensing up. Shit, not that question. Anything but that.

"You don't have to tell me," she said, playing with a string on the edge of the sleeping bag.

"No. It's okay." I couldn't just flat out say that I never dated anyone because I'd been in love with her for three years. Or explain that I'd tried to go out with other girls, but always broke it off after a night together because it had never been fair to them.

Though if I was honest, Tara wasn't the only reason I was single.

I sucked in a breath and spoke slowly, considering each word before I said it. "You know my parents were sent back to Mexico when I was thirteen. Worst day of my life. I got home from school and they were just...gone. No note or anything. No one knew what happened to them. My sisters wouldn't stop crying..." I closed my eyes against the flood of memories I usually kept buried deep. This was why I never talked about my past: it was too fucking hard. "We moved in with our *abuelita* and I had to become the man of the house overnight. We got through it, but taking care of my sisters, on top of school, the band, my job at the art supply store...it never left much time for dating."

"That makes sense." She slid her arms around my neck and pressed a soft kiss on my lips. I knew I could leave it at that, but I wanted to come clean with her. About this, at least.

"There's another reason." Shit, this was tough. I'd never told anyone this. The guys knew, but we never talked about it. "I did have one serious girlfriend in high school. Amanda. Pretty blond girl, like you. An aspiring actress. Parents were rich." I gritted my teeth and forced the last words out. "She got pregnant."

"Oh my god."

"We were so stupid. Mostly me. But I loved her, or thought I did anyway. I was going to do whatever it took to be there for her, to be a good father to our kid. I was saving up to buy her an engagement ring and everything. And then, like my parents, one day she was just gone."

Tara's arms tightened around me. "No."

"Her parents hated me. They tried to have me arrested when they heard I'd knocked her up. Didn't work, so they took her away, moved across the country so we couldn't be together. When I finally tracked her down she told me she'd lost the baby. She never talked to me again after that. It fucking killed me."

I could still remember the exact moment I'd learned I wasn't going to be a father after all. I'd expected to be relieved to not have the burden of a baby on top of everything else I was dealing with, but instead I'd been heartbroken. And it only got worse when Amanda had shut me out completely. After that, I'd resolved to never let anyone hurt me like that again.

I'd done a good job, until the other night with Tara, when I'd let my guard down. Somehow she'd managed to worm her way inside my heart—and all I could do was brace myself for when she broke it, too.

"I'm so sorry, Hector." She held me closer, gently stroking my hair. "No one should have to go through something like that."

I shrugged. "After that I stopped getting close to people. I don't let anyone in. It's just easier that way."

"You let me in."

"You were different. I didn't have to worry about you leaving because I never had you."

She kissed me on the corner of my mouth. "You have me now."

For another day, yeah. But after that? I was afraid to ask.

"Thank you for trusting me with that," she said.

She snuggled closer against me, but I held back from touching her. I'd let her see too much of me, opened myself up too far, and I had to shut it down somehow. Too many emotions were digging their way out and I had to bury them again. I needed to end the moment, to lighten things up and get the focus off of my past.

"Hey, I couldn't let you think there was anything wrong with me, with not having a girlfriend all these years. Believe me, there have been plenty of women here and there, but nothing serious."

Jesus, what a douchey line. I had to stop myself from cringing as I said it.

"Nothing serious," she said slowly. "Like this weekend?"

"Exactly."

Her face fell, and I wondered if she'd been hoping to hear something else. What did she want from me? A declaration of love? I couldn't do it. Not when I didn't know what would happen beyond tomorrow. Our future together was a black hole and I couldn't see what it held for us—and that terrified me.

I slid a hand around the curve of her ass, pulling her closer, fitting her against my body. "Hey, we're having fun, remember?"

She gave me a faint smile, but it didn't reach her eyes. "I remember. What happens at Comic-Con stays at Comic-Con."

I wished I'd never said that, but it was too late now to take it back. I pressed kisses to her neck and whispered, "No worries. No regrets. No complications."

She slipped her fingers under my shirt, along my abs. "In that case, we need to be having a *lot* more fun."

"Now?" I let out a sharp laugh. "We're surrounded by hundreds of people."

"Everyone is asleep." Her hand moved to the front of my jeans and popped open the button.

"Damn, you are one naughty girl." I looked around, but the others did seem to be sleeping. "Maybe we could have a *little* fun…"

She drew me in for a kiss and it was easy to lose myself in her, in the way she nibbled on my lip while unzipping my jeans, in the feel of her hand sliding into my pants.

"I just want to touch you," she said, between kisses. "No one will notice."

"Only if I'm allowed to touch you, too."

She didn't protest as I raised her shirt to seek out her breasts. She wasn't wearing a bra—she'd discreetly removed it before getting in the sleeping bag—and it gave me easy access to her already hard nipples. I loved the way her breasts felt in my hands, so full and soft, and the little sighs she made as I teased them were even better.

She helped me push her jeans down, kicking them off in the bottom of the sleeping bag. I grabbed her leg and draped it across my hip, opening her up to me. Her breathing sped up as I dipped a finger inside her panties, just along the edge. I inched closer. And closer. I traced every inch of her until she pressed against me and moaned, like she wanted more.

"Shhh," I said. "Don't want everyone to hear you."

"I can't help it," she whispered.

"Then I'll have to keep you quiet."

I crushed my mouth against hers, taking her little cries into my mouth as I slowly slid a finger inside her. She tightened her grip around my length and clutched at my neck, keeping my lips locked to hers. She stroked me up and down and sucked on my tongue with the same rhythm, driving me absolutely fucking insane. The girl knew how to use her hands. And her mouth. I couldn't help but imagine what it would be like if she used both of them together…. Maybe next time.

We touched each other without the desperation or ferocity from before. This time we were slow and gentle, taking time to learn each other. I found the spot that I'd already discovered made her lose control and she practically howled.

Someone moved in a nearby sleeping bag and we froze. We

stared into each other's eyes in the darkness, hearts pounding in sync, worried we'd been caught. Our greedy fingers were still on each other, but had paused in the middle of the action. We waited a minute, then two, but there was only silence. Until she giggled.

"Thought I told you to be quiet," I whispered.

I covered her mouth with my hand, which seemed to excite her even more. Her teeth dug into my skin while I began to rub her again and her fingers continued to work their magic on me.

We kept up a steady give and take, back and forth, with a slow build toward heaven. I wanted it to go on forever. Once we stopped we'd have to go back to reality, to our uncertain future. But here, like this, I could show her how much I loved her without having to admit it out loud.

When I knew I couldn't hold on much longer I increased my speed and pressure, making her arch her back. She clenched up around my fingers, making muffled sounds against my hand over her mouth, her entire body shuddering with pleasure. She kept pumping me as she lost control and I let her take me along with her, releasing myself into her hand.

We stroked each other until we were both completely sated, until exhaustion settled over us. I melted into her, my entire body warm and fluid as I cradled her against me. I never wanted to move again.

"Thank god you guys are done," Julie said, from the next sleeping bag. "I thought that would last all night. Nice job

Hector, and good for you Tara, but some of us are trying to sleep."

Tara laughed and covered her face with her hand.

"Eh, you're just jealous," I said to Julie.

"No kidding. I wish I had some of that right now. Hey, if you're up for sharing…"

"Definitely not," Tara said, tightening her arms around me. "He's all mine."

"Oh well, I tried," Julie said. "Get some sleep, love birds."

"Yours?" I asked Tara, kissing her neck. "I like the sound of that."

"Me, too." She snuggled against me, and I played with her hair while she settled in to sleep.

# CHAPTER FIFTEEN
# TARA

I woke in Hector's arms, blissfully warm against his hard body, while the sun rose over the convention center. Soon we'd go inside to watch all the big movie panels until it was time for our book signing. After that, we had the Masquerade and the afterparty and then one final night together before Comic-Con ended.

I had one more day to make my decision.

One more day with Hector.

I watched him sleep, admiring his long, dark lashes and his full, pouty lips. Careful not to wake him, I traced a finger over his face, along his eyebrows, his nose, his jaw. I drank in the sight of his broad shoulders, the way his dark hair curled over his forehead, the swell of his bicep around my waist. I wanted to memorize every inch of him before the day was over.

Last night he'd opened up to me for the first time ever, telling me things about his past I suspected he never revealed to anyone. My heart had broken when he'd told me about his high school girlfriend and the baby they'd lost. No wonder he had a hard time letting people in. Yet he'd let me in—for a few minutes, anyway. I'd felt closer to him than ever…and then he'd shut me out again. I'd only been able to bring him back to me by making things "fun" again.

From what he'd said, he didn't want anything serious—with me or any other girl. Yet those few moments when he did manage to let his guard down made me think he cared for me. He pushed me away and said we were just having fun, but then he said he wanted to be mine.

So which was it?

He opened his eyes and gave me a sleepy smile. "Hey, beautiful."

I pressed a soft kiss to his lips and he drew me closer against his body. Desire flickered inside me, like a red hot flame. I wanted to climb on top of him and ride him, despite being surrounded by people. Hector just brought out that side of me.

I brushed my mouth across his jaw. "*Te quiero*," I whispered, repeating his words from yesterday back to him. The ones that he'd said meant, "I want you."

He tensed up and swore under his breath, pulling away from me. "Jesus, Tara. Don't say that."

His reaction doused my lust like a bucket of ice water. I sat up, pulling my shirt down, feeling hurt and exposed. "Sorry."

"It's okay, just…." He took a deep breath and raked a hand through his already messy hair. After a second his body relaxed, and he flashed me a grin. "I want you, too. But when you speak like that it turns me on way too much, and we don't have time to do anything about that right now."

I nodded. He was right, of course. The rising sun cast a warm glow across the grass, where people were standing up and getting ready to go inside the convention center. Still, his reaction had been so extreme, it made me wonder if there was something else that was bothering him.

We spent the entire day together, sitting through the panels in Hall H with his friends, laughing and joking about the things we saw, gorging ourselves on bad convention food while checking out the cosplay. I was never eating another pretzel dog ever again after this weekend, that was for sure.

In between panels, Maddie told me about how she and Kyle became friends as freshmen in college, and how that led to her joining the band even though she'd been more of a classical musician before that. She had me cracking up with her story about how Jared had walked in on her playing his guitar at a party, and then showed up at her class to beg her to go on *The Sound* with his band.

Next, Alexis told me about how she and Kyle had gotten back together at a Battle of the Bands competition, and I discovered she was a photographer who was taking photos at Comic-Con for an entertainment news website. I also learned that Julie was a pre-med major but spent most of her free time designing clothes, and that Carla did modeling while getting a theater degree, loved fixing cars, and had a vintage Mustang.

Hector sat beside me the entire time, staying quiet while his friends did most of the talking. He was a steady presence, his arm resting on the chair behind me, his muscular thigh pressed against mine. It was a struggle to not touch him constantly, or grab him for a kiss in front of his friends, but I managed to restrain myself. Barely.

Our signing was scheduled near the end of the day in the same large, bright room as before. After a quick pit-stop in our hotel rooms to shower and change clothes, Hector and I made our way there together, chatting the entire time about how DC had better TV shows while Marvel had better movies. We pushed our way through the huge crowd and got to our section right on time—and it was packed. The line snaked back and forth in contained rows before bursting out and taking over the nearby wall, too.

"Oh, wow," I said, as we sat at our table behind our name tags. "I did not expect this."

"Same," Hector said. "I assumed everyone who wanted the book signed would have gotten it the other day."

Miguel joined us and set a box of Sharpies on the table, next to a huge stack of our books. "Big crowd, eh? All ready to start?"

I pulled out my own sparkly pens. "Ready."

We signed books quickly, with Miguel managing the line so it didn't become overwhelming but also moved at a brisk pace. It wasn't as stressful this time since we knew what to expect, and I was able to enjoy talking with the fans. Even Hector seemed more relaxed and chatty than normal, and he doodled silly sketches inside the books of people who asked him a good question—usually anything that didn't involve his band or *The Sound*.

I looked up to see who was next and saw Andy's smiling face. I glanced at Hector, but he was talking to Miguel and didn't notice my ex-boyfriend approach.

"Hey, Andy," I said, trying to keep my voice light. *Please don't let this be awkward*, I prayed.

"Hey!" He slid a copy of *Misfit Squad* in front of me to sign. "I'm so glad I could catch you at this signing. Look how many people there are!"

"I know, isn't it nuts?" I signed his book and added a personal thank-you note. "You didn't have to come though, you already have a copy of this."

"I had to see you signing books like a real author." He grinned. "Besides, I wanted a copy signed by both of you."

I slid the book to Hector. He kept his face neutral, but he gripped his Sharpie so hard I thought it might snap in half.

"Hey man, good to see you again," Andy said.

"You, too." He signed Andy's book with deep, sharp strokes, the pen squeaking as he wrote.

"Again, I'm really sorry I bailed on our dinner last night," I said. "I've just been so busy…"

"That's okay. Look how popular you are. I knew you would be."

Hector doodled a little cartoon devil inside Andy's book, but eyed us both with a surly look on his face as we spoke. The guy next in line cleared his throat.

"I'd love to talk to you for a minute," Andy said. "Maybe after your signing? We can grab that coffee."

"Sure, that would be fun."

"Great. I'll wait for you." He moved away and the next guy immediately replaced him with another copy of *Misfit Squad*.

I scribbled my name in more books than I could count. Miguel had to cap the line off, but even then we went well beyond our appointed time limit.

When the area finally cleared out, I shoved my sparkly pens in my bag and smiled at Hector. "That was even more fun than the first signing."

"Not as scary this time?"

"Nope. I knew what to expect. But now my hand hurts again."

"Let me help you." He took my hand in his and brought it to his lips, then started to massage it with slow, sensual strokes, never taking his eyes off mine.

I relaxed into his touch. "Mmm, you're so good with your hands."

"Come back to my room and I'll show you just how good."

"I approve of this plan." I wanted those hands all over me. And every other part of his body.

"Hey, Tara," Andy said, walking up to us. He frowned when he took in how close Hector and I were standing, how he held my hand against his chest. "Er, did I interrupt something?"

I jerked my hand away and took a step back, flexing my wrist. "No, he was just showing me a hand exercise. It got sore after signing so many books."

"Oh. Good."

The two guys gave each other long, silent looks. God, this moment was awkward. I stepped forward and hugged Andy, not knowing what else to do. "I'm so glad you're here."

"Me, too." He took his time to pull out of the hug, his hands lingering on my lower back. "Ready to get that coffee now?"

I checked the time and sighed. "I'm so sorry, Andy, but I can't. Please don't hate me, but the signing ran long, and now I have to get ready for the Masquerade. But, um, you should come to the Masquerade with us and hang out. Or if you can't make that, you can come to Hector's party after!"

I fished through my bag and handed him the flyer Hector had given me for the afterparty. Inviting Andy to either of these things wasn't very cool of me, since they'd been organized by

Hector and his friends, but I had to do *something* after ditching the poor guy over and over. I shot Hector a *please-forgive-me* look, but he was glaring across the room and I couldn't catch his eye. Shit. Was he mad?

"Okay," Andy said, examining the flyer. "Just as long as we get to hang out *some* time before Comic-Con is over."

"Of course! We will. For sure." I smiled at him, but caught Miguel waving me over. "Be right back."

I moved around the table, to where Miguel was stacking the empty boxes that had once held copies of our books. We'd sold out of them again. Go us.

"What's up?" I asked.

"I got a call from that producer Giselle Roberts. Well, her assistant actually. He said she was meeting with you and wanted early copies of the next two *Misfit Squad* books. What was that about?"

"I met with her yesterday. She loves the book and asked me to work for her as a writer on her new TV show."

"No way! That's great!" He rubbed his goatee. "I don't suppose she'd want to buy the film or TV rights to *Misfit Squad*, too?"

"She didn't mention it, but who knows? Maybe someday."

He nodded slowly. "We've been trying to get in with her for years, but she's so selective. This could be big for us. Really big. When do you start?"

"Um. I haven't accepted. I already have a job in the comics

division of Ostrich Books. I really want to work for Giselle, but…I don't know."

"Ah, yes. I forgot about that. Well, Black Hat supports you no matter what you choose, of course. But…I mean, it's *Giselle Roberts*."

His phone rang and he said, "Excuse me a second." He started speaking in Spanish to whoever was on the other line, and ended it with, "*Te quiero*." I jerked at the words, remembering what had happened this morning.

He shoved the phone back in his jeans. "Sorry about that. My wife wanted to know what time I was done here. She wants us to go to some Godzilla experience in the Gaslamp."

"That's okay." I chewed on my pinky nail. "This probably sounds like a weird question, but what does *te quiero* mean?"

"It means either 'I like you' or 'I love you' depending on who you're saying it to."

The world seemed to tip around me. *Love?* "It doesn't mean 'I want you?'"

"Nope. That's the literal translation, but it's not used that way. Why?"

"Oh, just…something I heard."

That must be why Hector freaked out this morning. He'd thought for a second I'd said that I loved him, and it had scared him before he realized what I'd meant. After what he'd told me last night it made sense—he was scared of getting close to anyone and getting hurt again.

But why had Hector lied about the translation? And which way had he meant it when he'd said it last night? Could he...? No. He must have been saying that he liked me.

My gaze traveled back to the other side of the table where Hector and Andy were chatting, their voices drowned out by the low buzz of the crowd. I couldn't see Hector's face but Andy was smiling, so it must not have been too going too terribly. The sight made me happy because it meant Hector was trying—for me.

All day long, I'd had an overwhelming sense that I belonged with Hector and his friends. I didn't want that feeling to disappear after Comic-Con. I would be crazy not to take the LA job. To be able to wake up next to Hector whenever I wanted— how could I say no to that? Or to Giselle Roberts and the opportunity of a lifetime?

It was terrifying, giving up the job I'd dreamed about for years. But in my gut this felt right.

I made my decision.

# CHAPTER SIXTEEN
## HECTOR

Tara ran off with Miguel, while Andy and I stood together in uneasy silence in the corner of the room. I crossed my arms and tried to look at anything but him.

Shit, the guy was wearing a polo shirt. It had a Batman symbol for the logo, but still—who wore a fucking *polo shirt* to Comic-Con?

And what the hell was he still doing here? She'd already said she couldn't get coffee with him. Of course, then she'd gone and invited him to the Masquerade and the afterparty. Bad enough I'd had to see them hug in front of me, now I'd be stuck watching them together all fucking night.

"So, uh." He gestured in Tara's direction. "Are you and her...you know..."

"No."

He exhaled in a rush. "Good, because I have something to tell her. And to ask her." He patted his pocket. "I just hope she says yes."

I grunted. "What, are you proposing?"

I'd meant it as a bad joke, but he smiled wider. "Yeah, I am. Do you think she'll say yes?"

"I..." Fuck. I could barely get the words out. He'd knocked all the air out of me without even hitting me. "I don't know."

"I think she will...the only reason we broke up is because we were moving to different cities, but I found a job in New York so we can stay together. I can't wait to tell her."

I stared at him. "You got a job in New York?"

"I did. I'm going to ask her to marry me so she'll see that I'm serious about us. That I want to make this work, whatever it takes."

I should have just handed him a knife to stab me with. It would have hurt a lot less. My fists clenched, my first reaction to punch his face in, to tell him to back off from my girl. But she wasn't mine, and I wasn't that kind of guy anymore.

Jesus, this guy was going to propose to Tara and I'd been inside her only hours ago. I was the other man, stealing Tara from Andy without even knowing it. Yeah, they'd been broken up at the time, but clearly it wasn't over. I'd seen the way she'd jerked away from me the second he'd arrived, and the way they hugged each other. She'd even admitted last night that she'd thought about marrying him.

I needed to end this thing with her immediately. I couldn't be the reason she said no to Andy or had any doubts about taking the New York job. I refused to get in the way of her happiness.

I'd been an idiot to hope for even a second that we could be anything more than friends. We'd had some "fun" moments together, but that was it. And I wanted her to be happy even if she wasn't with me, even if it killed me to see her with someone else. Hell, I'd done it for years and I'd survived. I could do it again. Maybe if she was engaged I could finally get over her.

Something burned at my eyes, like I was about to cry. But that was crazy. I *never* cried. Not since I was thirteen, anyway. I'd shed my last tears the day my parents were sent away, when I realized I had to toughen up and become a man for my sisters so they could cry as much as they needed. And now I had to suck it up and do what had to be done, for Tara.

"You should ask her tonight." Better to get the whole thing over with so we could all move on with our lives. She had to make her decision by tomorrow, so Andy didn't have any time to mess around.

"I will. Thanks, Hector." He shook my hand again. "You've always been a good friend to her."

"Yeah." A good friend. And that's all I would ever be.

"I have to admit, I've always been jealous of you, even though she told me over and over that there was nothing going on between you two. But I'm really glad you're in her life."

My throat closed up, as though his hands had tightened around it. No, there had never been anything going on between us. Our few days together at Comic-Con were the perfect reminder of why I kept people at arm's length and barricaded my heart. I'd made the mistake of letting Tara in and all it had done was get me hurt again. No more. I was done with that shit.

"Good luck tonight," I said.

"Thanks! Tell her I'll catch up with her later. I'm going to make some plans."

He vanished into the crowd and I rubbed my face, scrubbing off any lingering emotions. Wondering what the hell I'd just done. Dreading what I was about to do.

I wanted her to be happy even if she wasn't with me, even if it killed me to see her with someone else. Hell, I'd done it for years and I'd survived. I could do it again. Maybe if she was engaged I could finally get over her.

Tara bounced back to me with a bright smile. "Where'd Andy go?"

"He had to run, but he said he'll see you tonight."

Her smile wavered as she studied me. "What's wrong, Hector?"

I must not have hardened my face as much as I'd hoped. Hell, it was a miracle I'd kept it together this long. "Look, Tara. I've been thinking. We had fun over the past few days, but I don't want you to get the wrong idea."

She took a step back, confusion painted across her beautiful face. "The wrong idea?"

"This thing between us, it can't go any further. We're just friends. For Comic-Con we were friends with benefits. That's it." I shrugged as if it was nothing, as if forcing those words out wasn't the hardest thing I'd ever done.

She clutched the amethyst pendant around her neck, the one I'd given her. "So our nights together, everything you said…none of that meant anything?"

"Nope. It was just sex. Nothing more." I forced myself to maintain eye contact, even as her blue eyes filled with tears.

She blinked them back. "I don't believe you."

Jesus, why was she being so difficult? I'd told her before I couldn't do long distance, that I didn't want anything serious. If she wouldn't listen, I'd have to pull a card from Jared's player days, though I was about to be way more of an asshole than he'd ever been.

"Last night you asked me why I haven't had a girlfriend in years. You want to know the real reason? It's 'cause I sleep with girls a few times and then get bored. And it's time for me to move on."

A tear trickled down her face. "Hector, stop. I know you're not like that."

"Hell, yeah, I am. I never mentioned it 'cause why would I tell you about all the girls I've fucked? And trust me, there were a lot of them. With Jared taken, I'm in demand more than ever, and with the tour...well, let's just say I plan to fuck a *lot* more girls."

Everything I said was a lie and I hated myself a little more with each word, but it had to be done. I'd probably ruined my friendship with her too, but that was for the best. It'd be easier to forget her if she hated me. Easier to move on if she was out of my life completely. Even if it left my heart a barren wasteland.

She stared at me with tears dripping down her cheeks, and the sight made me want to take back everything I'd said. I was this close to confessing my real feelings for her and begging her to move to LA when she nodded slowly, wiping at her eyes. "If that's what you want."

"It is. I don't want anything serious, with you or anyone else."

"So what happens now? With us?"

"You take the New York job and we go back to being online friends. We keep working on *Misfit Squad* as we've always done. If you move to LA it will just be weird now, you know?"

"But...." She sucked in a breath, her voice faltering. "Please, Hector. Just tell me the truth. All this time, have you felt *anything* for me as more than a friend?"

I hesitated. This was my chance to be honest with her. To end the lies and try to win her back. But I shook my head.

"No. Never."

# CHAPTER SEVENTEEN
## TARA

I turned on my heel and slipped into the crowd without responding. I couldn't look at Hector for another second longer. I couldn't let him see me fall apart completely.

By the time I made it out of the convention center, I was running, the tears falling freely down my face. I blinked them back, trying not to let them escape, quickly wiping away the ones that did. It was stupid to cry over what he'd said. Over our two nights together. Over the future we would never have.

I didn't know what to do or where to go. Everything inside me hurt, like Hector had taken a scalpel to my heart and sliced out every piece that belonged to him. I'd made my decision, had been all ready to commit to a future with him, and then he'd crushed that dream into dust only seconds later. My entire life had been thrown into a tailspin and I wasn't sure how I could ever recover.

He'd said it meant nothing to him, but I didn't believe it. He'd said we could go back to being friends, but we both knew that wasn't going to happen. He'd said he wanted to sleep around, but that didn't sound like the Hector I knew. He wasn't that type of guy at all. In fact, he'd often complained about Jared doing exactly that. Had he changed his mind because of all the girls throwing themselves at him over the past few days? No. That didn't make any sense. There had to be something else going on.

I made it to the Gaslamp Quarter but stumbled into something out of a horror movie. Hundreds of people covered in fake blood and ripped clothes moaned and shambled slowly down the road. Great, a zombie walk. As if this moment couldn't get any worse.

I had to push my way through people calling for brains, but finally made it back to my hotel room. Once inside, my stomach clenched at the sight of my pirate costume. Earlier I'd rinsed it out and hung it up in the shower so it would be ready for tonight. But how could I go to the Masquerade now? I wasn't ready to face Hector so soon. Or maybe ever.

I texted Maddie: *Can't make it tonight. I'm so sorry.*

She immediately called me. I was tempted to ignore it, but

that would be rude. She'd never been anything but nice to me. I sighed and answered the phone.

"What's going on?" she asked.

"Hector..." I paused, trying to figure out how to explain what had happened. He hadn't dumped me per se, since we hadn't exactly been together. "I don't know what happened. One minute everything was great, and the next..."

"Come to our hotel room. We'll drink wine and eat ice cream and you can tell us the whole story."

"I don't know..." I wasn't sure I should talk to Maddie or the other girls about this. They were Hector's friends, after all. Our involvement should probably end here.

"Would you rather be alone? If so, I completely understand."

The tears threatened to return with a vengeance. Of course I didn't want to be alone. I wanted to spend my evening at the Masquerade with Hector and his friends, but now I couldn't do that. My other options were to sit in my hotel room and weep, or hang out with Andy. I didn't want to do either of those.

"Are you sure? It won't be weird since you're in the band with him?"

"Not at all. Trust me, if anyone knows how difficult Hector can be, it's me. When I joined the band, I was convinced he hated me, but I've gotten to know him a lot better since then. I'll help you figure out what's going on with him."

"Thanks, Maddie. I'll be there in a few minutes."

"Good. Oh, and Julie says to bring your pirate costume."

**F**ifteen minutes later I found myself in the hotel room Maddie was sharing with Carla and Julie. I'd collapsed onto one of their queen-sized beds, watching while they got ready for the Masquerade.

"We don't actually have any ice cream, but hopefully this will help." Maddie brought me a glass of red wine and sat on the other bed, eyebrows pinched together. She had on a nearly white blond wig that was done into pigtails. "Tell me exactly what Hector said."

I repeated the conversation as best I could, cringing when I remembered some of his harsher words, and was biting back tears by the end. It hurt just as much the second time and made even less sense.

The other night he'd said it had been a long time since he'd slept with anyone. Now he was trying to tell me he was a player? Something didn't add up. Was it because of the *te quiero* thing this morning? He hadn't brought it up again, but something had bothered him then. Or had Andy said something while I was talking to Miguel?

Carla leaned out of the bathroom, where she was doing her makeup. "I'm shocked. I didn't think Hector was that kind of guy."

"He's not," Maddie said. "Not even close. I've never even seen him flirt with a girl."

"So what's his deal?" Julie asked, from where she sat at the desk. She was in the middle of hand-sewing the hem of the red and black skirt Maddie was going to wear for her Harley Quinn costume.

"I wish I knew." I took a long sip of my wine and sighed. At least I had Maddie and her friends to talk to about the whole mess. I'd worried they would take Hector's side, or shut me out as soon as they heard he was done with me, but they were acting like they were *my* friends, too.

"Hang on." Maddie grabbed her phone.

"What are you doing?"

"Texting Jared. If anyone can find out what's going on with Hector, it's him."

# CHAPTER EIGHTEEN
## HECTOR

I returned to our hotel room and found Jared and Kyle getting ready for the Masquerade, their costumes already laid out across one of the beds.

"What's up?" Jared asked from the bathroom. His hands were in little plastic gloves and were slicking half of Kyle's head with hair dye.

"Nothing." I flopped on the bed, facing away from the bathroom door. I didn't want to talk to them. Maybe if I ignored them they'd leave me alone. Ha, fat chance.

"All done," Jared said to Kyle a few minutes later. "Have to wait twenty minutes now."

"I'll set a timer on my phone."

They both walked out of the bathroom and Jared sat on the edge of the other bed, eyeing me. "What's with you? Did your signing not go well?"

"It went fine."

"Did something happen with Tara?" Kyle asked, sitting next to his brother. One side of his head was covered in white hair dye, making it stick up all crazy. The other side was still black, but pinned back so it wouldn't get any color on it.

I turned away from them. "I don't want to talk about it."

Jared kicked my bed, making it shake. "Spit it out. What'd you do?"

Fuck, he was annoying. "I ended it, okay?"

"What?" Kyle asked. "Why?"

I let out a long groan and rolled onto my back, covering my face with my arm. "Her ex-boyfriend showed up with a wedding ring. He's moving to New York to be with her. I couldn't stand in the way of that."

"Oh, shit," Jared said.

"Does she *want* to get back together with him?" Kyle asked.

"I think so. She still has feelings for him. And she's been dreaming about that publishing job in New York her entire life. Ending it with her was the right thing to do."

The brothers were quiet, frowning at each other. Doing that near-telepathy thing they did. It was even more freaky because, if you ignored Kyle's wild hair, they looked so much alike.

"Does she know how you feel about her?" Kyle asked.

I grunted and rolled onto my side to face the wall again.

"I'll take that as a no."

"It doesn't matter. I was a total asshole. I told her I wanted to fuck a lot of girls now that we're popular and going on tour."

"Wow," Jared said. "Even I would never say that to a girl."

"No? Cause I was trying to channel you in that moment."

"Hey, despite what you think of me, I tried not to be an asshole to the girls I was with. I was up front with them that I wasn't after a relationship."

"Yeah? What about Becca?"

"I can't believe you're bringing that up again! First of all, that was a mistake I've apologized for a *hundred* times. You know I would go back and fix that if I could. Second, Becca knew what she was getting into. She just didn't want to accept it. And third, I'm not like that anymore. Give me a fucking break here."

"Knock it off," Kyle said. "Hector's just trying to piss you off so we'll stop asking him questions about Tara."

Jared drew in a long breath but said nothing. I felt bad for being a dick to him, but it was so nice to lash out about something, at *someone*, instead of sitting here wallowing in my own misery.

"Sorry, man," I muttered. I sat up and faced them, scrubbing at my eyes with my palms.

"Whatever." Jared checked something on his phone. "But you have to tell Tara how you feel. Otherwise you'll regret it."

Kyle nodded. "Jared's right. It's up to her to decide her future, but she needs to know you love her."

"I don't love her."

They both laughed. The exact same laugh at the same time, like they'd synchronized it. Damn, they were irritating. How had I put up with them for so many years?

I scowled at them. "You guys think you know everything about relationships now that you're both in love and on your way to two-point-five kids and a dog, but I don't need your advice."

"Sure you don't." Jared said, typing on his phone before looking up at me. "Now get your shit together so we can head out in approximately…fifteen minutes."

"I'm not going. Tara will be there."

"Maddie just texted me. Tara isn't going."

"Oh." Of course she wasn't going. Not after what I'd done. I'd probably never see her in person again.

Good. It was better when we'd only known each other online. Meeting in person had just fucked everything up. Andy would be proposing tonight, and then she'd be busy with him and her engagement ring and her new life. They'd get married and have babies like her parents wanted and everyone would be happy.

Everyone except me.

Whatever, I had other things that made me happy. My family. My band. My art. I didn't need anyone else.

I didn't need *her*.

# CHAPTER NINETEEN
## TARA

Alexis arrived with her costume in a bag under her arm while Carla and Julie did their makeup in the bathroom and Maddie and Jared texted back and forth. I had to explain the whole painful story all over again, and watched her green eyes get wider and wider with each word.

"I don't get it," she said. "That doesn't sound like Hector at all."

"Nope, not even close," Maddie said.

Alexis chewed on her lower lip as she considered. "Hector *is* pretty bad about expressing his emotions and stuff. Maybe he just...freaked out or something."

I sighed. "But why would he say all that stuff about sleeping around?"

"I don't know. He hasn't had a serious girlfriend in years. Probably not since we were in high school when...well, never mind that. But maybe he panicked because things between you two were moving so fast."

Maddie frowned at something she read on her phone. "Jared won't tell me what's going on. Bro code or something. But he says Hector is just as miserable as you are."

"I doubt Kyle will be any help either," Alexis said.

Maddie refilled my wine glass. "One thing I do know: Hector cares about you. A lot. If he's pushing you away it's probably for a reason."

"A reason..." I closed my eyes, replaying the memory again. "My ex-boyfriend Andy was talking to Hector right before it happened. Maybe he said something to set him off?"

"Could be," Alexis said.

I grabbed my phone and dashed off a text to Andy, asking what he'd said to Hector. But he just replied that he'd talk to me soon. "No help there. Ugh."

"Was there anything else that happened today?" Maddie asked. "Anything else Hector said?"

"He did tell me to take the New York job at the end..." I sat up straighter, sloshing a drop of wine on their comforter. "He must think that's what I really want! And that I was going to turn that job down because of him."

"Were you?" Julie asked, peeking out of the bathroom.

"Yes. Maybe. I don't know." I set my glass down and flopped back on the bed. "Oh, god, I'm so confused! I thought I knew which job to take, but now I'm not sure. Yes, a big part of the reason I chose the LA job was because Hector lives there, but now that seems so dumb. After today it will be weird for us to be in the same city. But if I pick the New York one I'll never have another chance with him."

Alexis sat next to me on the bed. "Why don't you tell us about the two jobs? But this time, forget Hector. Leave him out of it."

"Okay." I sucked in a breath and gave them a quick run-down about both positions and the kind of work I'd be doing at each one. I played with my necklace the entire time, and they listened patiently as I laid it all out for them.

"They're both great, but totally different," I added. "The LA job is scary because I feel so unqualified for it, but it's such an amazing opportunity. To work for Giselle Roberts, writing for a TV show like that...it would be incredible. But I've heard that TV writing jobs are high stress and not very stable." I was just pondering out loud now, but they let me talk it out without interrupting. "Whereas in the New York job I'd be more of an editor or producer, choosing and directing other people's projects and putting them together, shaping the future of the comics division at Ostrich Books. It would probably be just as high stress as the other job actually, and I wouldn't be writing anything myself either."

"Hmm. A tough decision," Maddie said. "Being an artist of any kind is a strange thing. Music for me is almost a...compulsion. An addiction. A form of madness. I can't imagine not doing it. It's always there, in the back of my mind, demanding my attention. Even on the days it's hard, even when I want to give up, I do it anyway, because I can't imagine *not* doing it. It's like breathing for me.

"And I think to make it in any kind of creative industry you have to feel like that or it's not worth it. It's just too damn hard otherwise. So my question for you is, are you *compelled* to write? Does it eat at your brain until you do it? Do you feel like you're missing something from your very soul when you don't? Or would you rather direct other writers, to guide them on their path and help them make their own stories even better? Both are equally important, it just comes down to what's right for *you*, and what you want to do with your life."

"I never thought about it that way." I chewed on one of my fingernails and considered what she said.

"Don't think about Hector," Alexis said. "Or whether you know people in a city or not. You'll meet people no matter where you live. Pick the job *you* want and everything else will work out the way it should."

Just like that, I knew what my decision had to be, and why I'd been so anxious about the New York job this entire time. It had nothing to do with the city, or with the people in it.

I was a writer. An artist. A *creator*.

I had to take the LA job. Even if Hector didn't want me. Even if his friends never talked to me again after today. Even if I was alone in the city forever. Because I wasn't doing it for him or for anyone else. I was doing it for *me*. This was what *I* wanted.

And, thanks to Maddie and Alexis, I had an idea that would make the job even better—assuming Giselle liked it, too.

I gave the girls each a hug. "Thank you so much. I know what to do now. I'm going to take the LA job."

"Glad we could help," Maddie said.

Alexis smiled. "Hey, if you need a place to stay in LA, let me know. My roommate just graduated and moved out."

Her offer was so tempting, but I shook my head. "Thanks, but I think I need to live on my own for a while. I've always relied so much on other people. It's time for me to be independent for a while. But I hope we can all stay friends, even if this thing with Hector doesn't work out."

"Of course!" Maddie said. "You're one of us now. One of Gotham's most wanted."

"Um, I never said I was going to the Masquerade."

Julie sank down on the other side of me, now wearing a long red wig. "Of course you are. You're not going to let a stupid man ruin your weekend, are you?"

"Julie's right," Carla said, dropping onto the bed beside Maddie. "You *have* to join us for the Masquerade. She's got your costume all ready and everything."

"I don't know. Hector will be there…" I looked around at the four girls surrounding me. They barely knew me, yet they were all on my side, completely supportive of my decisions and trying to make me feel better—like real friends should be. I didn't want to let them down. But I was scared to see Hector again so soon, too.

Julie wrapped an arm around me and squeezed. "Girl, when Hector sees you in the costume I've put together he'll *beg* you to come back to him."

# CHAPTER TWENTY
## HECTOR

After Kyle's hair was done and they rinsed out the white dye in the sink, we walked to the convention center to meet the girls. Comic-Con had a rule that you couldn't wear your costumes for the Masquerade before the competition, so we all had to finish getting dressed backstage. But when we arrived I wanted to turn around and run out—because Tara was there. She was talking with Carla and had her back to me, but I would recognize that blond hair and perfect ass anywhere.

"Thought you said she wasn't coming," I growled.

"Oops." Jared shrugged, flashing a devious grin. "She must have changed her mind."

"You planned this, didn't you, you son of a…"

I shut up when Maddie ran over to us with a big smile on her face. She ruffled Kyle's black and white hair. "Nice job."

"Why thank you," Jared said, giving her a quick kiss.

"Hector…" She gave me a disappointed look from behind her glasses that made me feel like an even bigger asshole than I already did. Tara must have told her everything. "Don't even think about leaving. And be nice."

What did that mean? I wasn't going to start anything. Hell, if it were up to me I'd be back at the hotel already. The absolute last thing I wanted to do was be around Tara knowing I couldn't have her.

She turned toward me and, even with the crowd rushing around us, all I saw was the cobalt blue of her eyes. She paled and quickly looked down, tucking a strand of golden hair behind her ear. Her face looked puffy, like she'd been crying, yet was still the most beautiful thing I'd seen all day.

Julie immediately whisked our group to the backstage area where we had to get ready. I didn't get a second to talk to Tara or even catch her eye. And who was I kidding—there was no way in hell she'd want to talk to me anyway. I was shocked she'd come at all, after what I'd done. She must not have spoken to Andy yet or they would be together, celebrating their perfect future. I hated that I'd hurt her and was unable to apologize, at the very least. Maybe the guys were right, and I should tell her how I feel. But that would only complicate things more.

Backstage was pure chaos, with everyone in the competition scrambling to get their costumes on. We pulled our clothes out of wardrobe bags and it became a mad rush to get them on as fast as possible.

Julie darted back and forth between us, making sure our outfits were okay, fixing any last minute emergencies, and making any tweaks to the fitting. She was cosplaying as Poison Ivy with a bright red wig, a leather choker with ivy leaves, and a green plaid dress with metal buckles that was so tiny I'm not sure it actually qualified as a dress. Carla helped her with hair and makeup, dressed as Catwoman in a black leather jacket with spikes all over it, pants with jagged slices cut through them, and cats-eye sunglasses perched on her head.

We were Gotham's finest villains with a punk twist. If all of Batman's enemies had formed one giant rock band, that would be us. Julie had put the entire thing together, designing and sewing many of the clothes herself, taking inspiration from the traditional comic book costumes for each character but giving them a tough, modern edge. I had to admit we all looked pretty fucking awesome.

The others had made me go as Bane, in a black military-style vest, black cargo pants covered in zippers and straps, and combat boots. Not too different from what I wore on stage, though I missed my Villain Complex hat.

"Looking good," Julie said, inspecting my costume. "But where's your mask?"

I crossed my arms. "I'm not wearing the mask."

"You have to wear it. Without it you just look like a muscular guy in black."

"Fine with me."

She gave me a look that didn't leave any room for argument. I groaned and grabbed the stupid bandana. It was black and white and went over my mouth and nose, a more everyday version of Bane's mask. "Fine."

"Mmm, you are the sexiest villain ever," Jared said to Maddie, yanking her close and kissing her. They were dressed as Gotham's most notorious couple, with Jared as the Joker in dark purple pants covered in patches and chains, a black t-shirt that said "Ha ha ha" in green letters, and a studded leather jacket. Maddie was Harley Quinn with a short, sexy dress that alternated between red and black under a jacket like Jared's, plus matching knee-high tights and boots. Her look was complete with a light blond wig done in pigtails, a leather collar around her neck, and her signature black-rimmed glasses.

"No kissing!" Julie snapped at them. "You'll ruin your makeup."

Kyle had his arms around Alexis and looked like he was about to break that rule, too. He was going as Two-Face with his wild hair and a costume that had one side in black leather with spikes and chains, the other side smooth, simple, and white. Beside him, Alexis looked super hot as a genderbent version of the Riddler, wearing a tight green top with question marks all over it, black cut off shorts, purple sunglasses and boots, and a tiny bowler hat over her long red hair.

I enjoyed checking out all the girls in their costumes, but the only one that made me absolutely speechless—and instantly hard—was Tara. Julie had somehow pulled off an amazing last minute costume, transforming Tara into a female version of the Penguin. She was in all black and white with a leather mini-skirt, thigh-high fishnets, and those killer leather boots that showed off her shapely legs. She had on that corset from her pirate costume that brought back all sorts of erotic memories, along with a bowtie at her neck, fingerless biker gloves, and a top hat.

She looked so hot I wanted to bend her over and take her from behind like I'd done last night. Or pin her against the nearest wall and wrap her legs around me like I'd done the other night. But neither of those was going to happen ever again. I had to accept that we were over.

As we got ready, she stayed as far away from me as she could. The other girls hovered around her, keeping her busy at all times, like they were protecting her from me. I was glad they'd become friends and that she with us tonight, even if it meant I had to spend hours in her presence, trying not to go crazy knowing Andy could show up and propose at any minute.

Once Julie approved all of our costumes, we were taken to another room with a panel of judges. They had us pose for pictures and inspected our costumes. I reluctantly wore my Bane bandana the entire time even though it was uncomfortable as shit. I hoped Maddie and Jared appreciated it. I liked Julie too, but for my best friend and the girl who'd turned his life around? I'd dress up in whatever the hell they wanted.

After the judging and photos we were sent backstage again and told to wait until it was time to go on. Inside Ballroom 20 the show was starting, but we could only make out muffled microphone voices and music. There were no chairs backstage, so we leaned against a wall and surveyed the other costumes around us.

I couldn't stop looking at Tara. Every second I was near her was pure torture. I had to say something. I had to apologize to her. I couldn't leave things the way they were, even if all I did was try to repair our friendship. The thought of not having her in my life at all was just too unbearable.

But right as I was about to summon the courage to talk to her, she jumped up and walked away, clutching her phone in her hand.

# CHAPTER TWENTY-ONE
## TARA

Andy texted me that he was inside the convention center, so I told him to meet me at the room we were all stuck in. He couldn't get inside since he wasn't part of the Masquerade, and I had to get a bathroom pass from one of the volunteers to slip out for a few minutes. How annoying.

I'd been dying to speak with Andy ever since Hector had flipped out on me, hoping he could shed some light on what had happened. All night I'd been tempted to say something to Hector, but wasn't sure what. I wanted to tell him about my decision, but I was still too upset with him. If he wasn't ready to apologize for being a jerk then I had nothing to say to *him* either.

The convention center had thinned out a lot now that everyone at Comic-Con was off to either grab dinner, crash in their hotel rooms, or head to other events and parties. I found Andy leaning against the second floor railing, staring down at the lobby. He'd changed clothes from when I'd last seen him, wearing a black button-up shirt over dark blue jeans, his blond hair slicked back. He looked handsome but out of place, especially next to me.

He eyed me up and down, obviously surprised by my costume. "Wow. You look…striking."

Was that a compliment? I couldn't tell. Hector would have just said I looked "smoking hot" or something. God, I missed him. I missed what we'd almost had.

"Thanks," I said, adjusting my top hat, which kept threatening to fall off despite the bobby pins Carla had stuck in it. "What did you want to talk about?"

He gestured for me to follow him and we moved down the hall and around a corner, to where it was a little more quiet. There wasn't really any privacy in a place like Comic-Con though. I hoped he would be fast; I wasn't sure how long I had before we would be sent on stage.

"I don't have much time," I said. "What's going on? Did you say something to Hector earlier?"

"I wanted to do this over dinner, but you've been so busy. But it doesn't matter. I have some great news." He took both my gloved hands in his, and I let him. "I'm moving to New York."

I blinked at him, the words not registering for a second. "What happened to the job in Dallas?"

"I changed my mind and found a job in New York so I can be with you." He gave me a huge smile and took a step closer, so we were only inches away. "Isn't it great? We can even get an apartment together. I know you were worried about moving there on your own, and now you don't have to."

I stared into his warm, hazel eyes, and for a second I was tempted. Maybe it was my destiny to take the New York job and get back together with Andy. Things with him had always been good. Our relationship had been easy, comfortable, and practical. We'd been together a year and had never fought. We'd always had fun together. He was great in bed. Not Hector great, but pretty close.

And working in publishing in New York was my dream job. It was more stable than the LA one, and didn't have the complication of being in the same city as Hector.

Being with Andy would be easier than being alone, right?

I could see my future stretch out before me…and it wasn't bad at all. Andy didn't set me on fire from the inside out like Hector did, but maybe that was better. In the end, Hector had only burned me.

Hector didn't want me. Andy did.

I didn't know how to respond. My head said one thing and my heart said another. "I'm just…I'm shocked."

"I know it's a lot to take in. But the last few days without you have been miserable. I'll do anything to win you back." He got down on one knee in the middle of the hallway and held out a small jewelry box. "I love you, Tara. Now that we're both going to be in the same city, I know we can make it work. Will you marry me?"

# CHAPTER TWENTY-TWO
## HECTOR

"**W**hat are you doing? Go after her, you idiot," Jared said.

I crossed my arms. "Why? What's the point?"

Kyle rolled his eyes. "The point is that you love her, dumbass. And you need to make this right, before it's too late."

"It's better off this way."

Jared draped an arm across my shoulders. "Hector, we've been friends a long time, and I know what a stubborn ass you can be. I also know that you're one of the most sensitive guys in the world, even though you'll never admit it. Now get over yourself and tell her how you feel before she gets engaged to some other guy. If she turns you down, at least you tried. But if you don't do it, you'll spend the rest of your life wondering what could have happened."

"Shut up," I growled.

"Face it, you're a big, grumpy teddy bear," Kyle said, grinning. "And for some crazy reason Tara seems to think that's hot."

"She's going to marry Andy. I don't want to get in their way."

Maddie lightly placed a hand on my arm. "But Hector, she doesn't want to be with Andy. She loves *you*."

Impossible. Someone as perfect as Tara loving me? No fucking way. She was sunlight on warm summer days and I was a starless night with cold, stiff rain. She could have any guy she wanted. Why in hell would she choose me?

"She doesn't love me."

"She does. Trust me on this one." Maddie sounded so confident I almost believed her.

Almost.

But if Tara really did love me that changed everything.

My whole life was heavy and there were only three things that made it lighter: drawing, drumming, and her. I was good at building walls, not tearing them down. But for her? I'd try my hardest. For her, I'd give this long distance thing a shot. No matter what job she took, no matter what city she lived in, I'd move mountains to be with her.

Unless I was too late already.

Jesus, what had I done? I'd told her I didn't feel anything for her as more than a friend. I'd told her to take the New York job. Hell, I'd practically shoved her into Andy's arms. I had to find her and tell her how I felt before I lost her forever.

"Where did she go?" I asked.

Maddie gestured to one of the doors. "I saw her get a bathroom pass, so she must be right outside."

Jared thumped me on the back. "Good luck."

I rushed past them and to the volunteer at the door, snatching the bathroom pass from her hand without a word. Tara wasn't right outside, but she had to be around here somewhere. I headed in the direction of the closest bathroom to look for her, preparing a speech inside my head. Trying to come up with something that would convince her she belonged with me and not Andy.

But when I turned the corner, I saw them. Tara's back was to me so I couldn't see her face, but in front of her Andy was on bended knee, holding out a ring. The sight tore through me like a grenade going off at my feet, flaying every inch of my heart with shrapnel. I could only watch in stunned silence for a beat, before turning on my heel and walking away, choking on the words I'd never be able to say to her.

I was too late.

# CHAPTER TWENTY-THREE
## TARA

Andy flicked open the jewelry box, revealing an engagement ring. I gasped and covered my mouth with my gloved hand, too stunned to speak. He stared up at me with a hopeful expression on his face, and a few people stopped outside the bathroom to watch the scene unfold.

He waited for an answer, but I didn't have one. My eyes were locked on the box with the ring I'd wear for the rest of my life if I said yes. Inside was a small diamond solitaire on a gold band.

A *gold* band.

I clutched at the amethyst pendant around my neck, with its sterling silver chain. I was allergic to gold. Hector knew that.

After a year, how could Andy not?

I'd told him before that I wasn't ready for marriage. We'd broken up and I'd never hinted I wanted to get back together with him—and now he was *proposing*? Why in the world would he think that was a good idea? Especially at Comic-Con, of all places.

No, I couldn't do this. I couldn't accept a life that wasn't *bad*. I wanted a life I woke up every day feeling grateful for and excited about—even if the path to get there was difficult. And I didn't want a love that was easy, comfortable, or practical. I wanted a love that set my every nerve on fire, that made me forget what day it was, that breathed life back into me.

That life was in LA.

That love was Hector.

"I'm sorry Andy, but I'm not moving to New York."

"You're not?" His hand faltered, dropping to his side, but didn't put the ring away.

"No. I'm taking a job in LA."

"I see." He nodded slowly. "Okay. That's not ideal, but we can make it work. I'll find a job there instead."

"No!" I blurted out. "Andy…even if we live in the same city, it's over."

He stood up and shoved the jewelry box in his pocket. "I don't understand. We broke up because we were moving to different cities, but that isn't a problem anymore. We can still be together."

I sighed. "That wasn't the only reason we broke up."

"But…I love you. You said you loved me. We've been together for a year. I don't get it. What did I do wrong?"

"You didn't do anything wrong. You were a great boyfriend. It just…wasn't enough. I'm sorry."

"It's him, isn't it?" Andy asked, his eyes narrowing. "All this time, you've been in love with Hector. I tried not to be jealous of your relationship with him. I tried to give you space because you said you were just friends. But you've been cheating on me with him, haven't you?"

"No! It was never like that between us."

Except now I realized it kind of was.

Hector was the one I dreamed about when I went to bed and the one I woke up thinking about. He was the first person I rushed to share both good and bad news with. The person I trusted more than anyone else in the world. The person I missed when I didn't talk to him for even a few hours. The person who made me smile even on my darkest days.

We'd never had anything romantic until this week—but in my heart it had *always* been him.

I realized now I'd been in love with Hector for years, I'd just never allowed myself to admit it because we couldn't be together. I'd tried to deny it, tried as hard as I could to fall in love with Andy, but the person I wanted to spend all my waking hours with had always been Hector. Andy and the guys before him had just been substitutes, at least subconsciously. Once I'd finally met

Hector in person, it made me realize just how much I'd been missing with everyone else.

"Just give me another shot," Andy said. "Please. I'll do whatever you want."

My eyes watered because I knew this was going to hurt Andy and because this hurt me, too. It was hard to say goodbye to someone who had once been so important in my life, but I was confident in my decision. There had been nothing wrong with Andy or with our relationship—but there hadn't been anything special about it either. We were together because we'd been together for months and got along great and because change was hard. That's why graduation and moving to new cities had been the perfect excuse to break it off.

But even if I didn't end up with Hector, I couldn't be with Andy. I'd rather be alone than with a guy who wasn't right for me, and it wouldn't be fair to him to keep leading him on. As difficult as it was, this had to end now—for good.

"I'm sorry, Andy, but I can't. You need a girl who will love you the way you deserve and I am just not that girl. I'm so sorry."

He bowed his head and looked so dejected I wanted to hug him. "I guess I knew it was over but I thought...I don't know. I wanted to put everything out there and see if I could make it work between us. I even asked Hector and he told me to do it. Guess we were both wrong..."

My heart stopped, like the entire world had fallen out from under my feet. "Hector knew you were going to propose?"

"Yeah, I told him about it at your signing. Why?"

"Oh my god. It all makes sense now." All the pieces connected in my head, making me dizzy. Hector's sudden reversal. His lies about how he wanted to sleep around. His insistence on me taking the New York job. He must have thought I still had feelings for Andy, and believed he was doing the right thing by pushing me away.

"I need to get back," I said to Andy, giving him a quick hug. "Take care of yourself, okay? You're a great guy, and I know you'll find the right girl for you soon."

"Yeah. Thanks." He muttered the words and I hated that it had to end this way between us. I hoped he could forgive me and move on, and that maybe one day we could be friends again.

But right now, I had to find Hector.

# CHAPTER TWENTY-FOUR
## HECTOR

It was done. Tara was engaged.

And somehow I had to get over her.

I drew in a ragged breath. I knew I should return to my friends and get ready to go on stage, but I needed to be alone for a few minutes first. The patio outside Ballroom 20 had fit the bill perfectly since it was cool, dark, and, most importantly, empty.

I leaned against the balcony and stared across the marina at the twinkling lights on the water. The sun had set, but I could make out the pirate ship we'd been on the other night, a large cruise ship, and even a huge Navy battleship. On the grass below me, people were already camping out for tomorrow's Hall H panels, like we'd done last night.

Comic-Con was almost over. Tomorrow, Tara would fly back to Boston to prepare for her future in New York. I would get on a tour bus and start working with the band on songs for our album. Everything would return to the way it was supposed to. I just wished it didn't feel so fucking *wrong*.

"Hector!"

Tara's voice was breathless, like she'd been running. I turned, taking in her flushed cheeks and disheveled hair. She looked as beautiful as ever, and it made my heart clench. What was she doing here? Why wasn't she with Andy?

This was it. My last chance to tell her how I felt. Jared and the others were right—I would regret it forever if I didn't try to fight for her. I was done pretending, done making excuses, done lying and keeping secrets. I'd just throw everything out there and if she turned me down, well, things couldn't be any worse than they were now.

"Tara, I—"

"Hector, why—"

We both spoke at once and then shut up. I held up a hand to stop her. "Please, I need to tell you something before you marry Andy."

She opened her mouth like she wanted to interrupt, but I kept going. I had to, otherwise I'd never get the words out.

"Tara, I love you." Damn, it felt good to say that out loud

after keeping it a secret for so long. "I've loved you for years. From the very beginning, it's always been you."

Her eyes widened, sparkling with starlight. "Hector—"

"You asked me why I haven't had a girlfriend in a long time, and I lied to you twice. The real reason is because my heart belongs to you. I haven't been able to even look at another girl for years." I took a step toward her, more nervous than I'd been in ages, yet unable to stop the confession now that I'd started. "I know it's too late, but I had to tell you how I really feel about you. If you still want to marry Andy, I'll accept that and we never have to talk about this again. We can go back to being friends, if that's what you want. But if you do feel something for me, then I'm willing to do the long distance thing. I'll do whatever it takes so I don't lose you. These past few days with you have been the best in my life, and I can't let you go home without—"

"Hector, stop!" She yelled the words but she was smiling, her face radiant. "I told Andy no."

"You…you said no?"

"I turned him down." She wrinkled her pretty nose. "He got me a gold ring."

"But you're allergic to gold."

"I know!" She smiled wider, gripping the necklace I'd given her. "But that's not the only reason I said no."

I couldn't breathe, couldn't think, couldn't dare to hope. "It's not?"

"No. I don't love him." She closed the distance between us,

sliding her arms around my neck, looking up at me with shining eyes. "I love *you*, Hector."

For a long beat all I could do was stare at her, too shocked to respond. Then I hauled her against me and captured her mouth with mine. She responded eagerly, locking her fingers in my hair, fitting her body against me. It was a kiss full of love and hope, a kiss that promised happy endings, a kiss that sucked all the darkness out of me and replaced it with light. Her light.

I rested my head against her forehead. "I never thought I would hear you say those words."

"I didn't realize it until this week, but I've been in love with you for a long time. I should have figured it out sooner."

"No, *I* should have told you how I felt sooner."

"It doesn't matter. We're together now." Between each word she pressed small kisses all over my mouth, my cheek, my jaw. "Oh, and I'm taking the LA job."

"You are?"

"Yep. Not because of you, though, but because I want it more than the other job."

I laughed and picked her up, spinning her around once before setting her on the ground and kissing her again. My heart was so full it nearly hurt. She loved me and she was moving to LA. I didn't know how it was possible, but I wasn't going to argue it. If she wanted to be with me I was never letting her go.

"There you are," Julie said, behind us. "I hate to ruin your happily ever after, but it's time for us to go on stage. And you better not have messed up your makeup or, god forbid, your costumes."

Oh right. The Masquerade. I'd forgotten about that.

"Sorry," Tara said, blushing. "We'll be right there."

We followed Julie backstage, holding hands the entire time, and the group whooped and cheered when they saw us enter together. I scowled at them, or tried to, at least. It was hard to don my usual grumpy face at the moment.

Julie checked our costumes and makeup, clucking at Tara for messing up her hair and lipstick. They fixed it, I wrapped the bandana around my face, and then it was time to go on stage.

Ballroom 20 wasn't as big as the massive Hall H but had a grander feel to it. Aisles and aisles of red chairs had been set up across the scrolling carpet in front of the stage, and screens hung from the ceiling at regular intervals so everyone could see what was happening, even in the back.

Our song "Behind the Mask" started playing through the speakers, and the Comic-Con volunteers waved us on. We went out in pairs, with Alexis and Kyle first, in their Riddler and Two-Face costumes. They strolled onto the stage and posed while the music played behind them. Tara and I were next, as the Penguin and Bane, and I lifted my bandana to give her a quick kiss before we joined them out there. Next up were Carla and Julie cosplaying as Catwoman and Poison Ivy, walking onto the stage like they owned it. Finally, Jared and Maddie emerged as the Joker and Harley Quinn. When they got to the middle he took her in his arms and dipped her on the stage, pulling her in for a kiss while the audience cheered and clapped.

For a few beats we posed while the announcers read out our names, and then our time was up and we walked backstage again. It all happened so fast, but I was used to that kind of chaos from our concerts and from being on *The Sound*. Still, it was always a rush to be in front of an audience, whether it was playing drums or doing something like this. And this time it was even better because I had Tara at my side.

# CHAPTER TWENTY-FIVE
## TARA

After we exited the stage we were directed to the press area to pose for photos as a group in front of a white background with the Comic-Con logo all over it. We stood there for a good fifteen minutes or so before they brought the next group up, who were all dressed in extremely detailed *Bioshock* costumes.

A Comic-Con volunteer ran up to us. "Which one of you is Julie Hong?"

Her eyebrows shot up. "That's me."

"Your group won an award." The man checked his paperwork. "The, ah...*Behind The Seams* Award?"

"What?" Julie shrieked.

"*Behind The Seams*, like the reality TV show?" Alexis asked.

"That's the one," the guy said. "You did enter to win that, yes? It was an optional category…"

"Yes, I definitely entered." Julie fanned herself with her hand. "I won? Seriously?"

"You did. You have to come on stage and accept during the awards ceremony at the end of the show, but the sponsor wants to talk to you first."

"No freaking way!" Julie turned to us, her eyes like saucers. "You guys, can you believe it?"

Maddie hugged her. "I believe it. Your costumes were amazing!"

We all crowded around Julie and offered congratulations. I gave her a hug too, and she squeezed me back as hard as she did the others.

"Thanks, everyone," she said. "I couldn't have done it without you. It was originally just going to be me, Maddie, and Carla, but it became so much better after the rest of you joined us."

"You did all the hard work," Kyle said. "We just had to stand there and look pretty."

"Easier for some of us than others," Jared said, winking.

Julie laughed and wiped at her eyes. "But seriously. I wouldn't have won without your help."

"We'll have to celebrate at the afterparty," Hector said, wrapping an arm around me.

"Definitely," I said. I was so happy to be part of this group and so excited for my future with them. My new friends. My new love. My new life.

Giselle Roberts appeared next to our group, with her blond hipster assistant at her side. "Sorry, am I interrupting?"

Julie's eyes flared as she recognized who had joined us. "Oh wow, *you're* the sponsor? I mean, of course you are! You created *Behind The Seams*. I just…I didn't expect…"

Giselle gave one of her bubbly little laughs. "I am the creator and producer, yes, and I'm delighted to offer you a spot in our upcoming season as part of the award, if you're interested. The only thing is it starts filming next week and lasts a few weeks, culminating in New York Fashion Week in early September, so I'll understand if you can't make it. But I was impressed with your villain-themed punk rock collection tonight, and I think you would do really well on the show. I'd love to have you on it."

"This is the most exciting thing that's ever happened to me!" Julie said. "Um, yes! I would love to be on the show. I'm on summer break until the middle of September, so I can definitely make it."

"Perfect. My assistant here will take down all your information and contact you after Comic-Con with all the details."

Julie threw her arms around the woman. "Thank you, thank you, thank you. I won't let you down, I promise!"

"I'm sure you won't." She pulled back and caught my eye with a smile. "Hello, Tara. I didn't realize you were part of this group. I swear, I didn't pick Julie as the winner for that reason."

"I would never think that," I said. "But could we talk alone for a minute?"

"Of course."

We moved away from the group and into a quieter corner of the backstage area. Her assistant stayed behind, jotting down Julie's contact information.

"Have you come to a decision?" Giselle asked.

"I have. And I want to take the job."

"Great! I never doubted you would."

"There's just one thing I want to run past you." I resisted the urge to bite my fingernails and instead gripped my amethyst pendant. It had always given me strength, and I realized it was because it made me feel like Hector was with me even when he wasn't. "I think you should do a comic book tie-in for the show. You could have one come out each week online and use it to give origin stories for different superheroes and villains, or show superheroes in different parts of the world and what they're up to. It would make the world of your TV show feel so much bigger, and be a fun thing for your fans. Plus it might bring in more of the hardcore comic book readers."

She tapped a finger against her lips as she listened to my spiel. "I like this idea. A lot. So you'd write this for me?"

"I would, if you're open to it."

"Hmm. I think that could work. I want you to help with the

individual episodes, too, though. I want you to be a vital part of the team, shaping the direction of the show for as long as it's on. But you could split your time between the two projects." She nodded, her eyes far away as the gears in her head turned. "Yes, I love this idea. You'll be even more involved this way. Now we just need an artist or two…"

I smiled. "I know the perfect guy."

# CHAPTER TWENTY-SIX
## HECTOR

After Julie got her award and the show ended we headed back to our hotel for the villain afterparty Jared had set up. I just wanted to sneak up to Tara's hotel room, but everyone insisted we stay and celebrate for a while.

The club was small and had a goth look to it, with chandeliers dripping with red lights, black velvet walls, and leather booths. The bar was lit in an eerie blue and the drinks all came in glowing skull glasses. Jared had talked extensively with the DJ earlier to make sure the music met his approval, and he must have done a good job because the club was packed with people dancing, wearing costumes ranging from Maleficent to

Loki to Green Goblin. We were all still in our costumes too, the eight of us crammed into the largest booth in the corner.

Jared raised his glowing glass in a toast. "Julie, let's hope your reality TV show experience goes much smoother than ours did."

"Hey, it didn't turn out so badly," Maddie said, giving him a playful shove.

"Very true." He raised his glass higher. "To Julie!"

We all toasted as a group and took a sip of whatever we were drinking. I chugged my beer, feeling content for the first time in as long as I could remember. Good friends, good drinks, and good music. Not to mention a beautiful girl at my side who loved me. What more could I want?

"So you're really going on that show?" Alexis asked.

"I think so," Julie said, laughing. "My parents won't like it, but…yeah, I'm going to do it. Why not?"

"You should get Carla to be your model," Kyle said.

"Hey, that's a good idea. What do you say, Carla?"

She tilted her head and considered. "I'll have to think about it."

A blonde walked into the club wearing a tank top that read, "This *is* my slutty costume." I straightened up. "Oh, shit. Becca is here."

"Your former bassist?" Tara asked.

Jared shrugged. "Well, I *did* invite her."

I kept my eye on her as she perched at the bar. "Just as long as she doesn't cause any trouble."

"Nah, I think she really has changed," Kyle said.

"We'll see."

"Come on, let's dance," Alexis said, dragging Kyle out of the booth.

Julie downed the rest of her glowing drink. "Time for me to find a guy I can bring back to our hotel room."

"Hey, that's my hotel room, too," Carla muttered.

"And mine," Maddie said.

"Nah, you'll be in my room all night," Jared said, nuzzling her ear. "I have all sorts of naughty things planned for you in that costume. And I still have some of that whip cream…"

Tara leaned against me and whispered, "Sounds like you'll be spending the night in my room."

"Can't complain about that." I slid an arm around her back and pulled her in for a kiss.

"Check out that guy in the Rocket Raccoon costume," Julie said, nodding toward the bar.

"Does that even count as a costume?" Maddie asked. "He's wearing an orange shirt with raccoon ears and a tail. That's not trying very hard."

Julie stood up and smoothed out her dress. "When he looks like that, who cares?"

"It's just…not right," Carla said. "He's hot, but then he has ears. And a tail."

"I know. That just makes it hotter." She grinned and slipped off to flirt with him. Carla trailed behind her, shaking her head.

The group split up, with each of us going our separate ways inside the club. Tara and I stayed in the booth while she told me about her idea for a comic book related to Giselle's show. She'd suggested that I do the art, but I wasn't sure how I'd juggle the band, *Misfit Squad*, and another project on top of that. I told her I'd consider it. At least I was finally making enough money from my music and my art that I wouldn't have to go back to my job at the art supply store after the tour.

On stage, Maddie and Jared started belting out "Don't Stop Believin'" by Journey, beginning the karaoke portion of the night. They both had amazing voices and alternated the verses but harmonized on the chorus, sending little chills down my spine. From the way they sang together, working the stage with their eyes locked on each other, it was obvious how much they loved each other.

As they sang, Alexis and Kyle danced close, lightly brushing their lips together like they were in their own world and nothing existed around them.

And this time, I wasn't jealous.

"Never thought I'd see the Joker and Harley Quinn singing *that* song," I said.

Tara smiled as she watched them. "They're so cute together."

"I know. Hard to believe that a few months ago Jared would sleep with anything with boobs and Maddie was too shy to even play guitar on stage."

Tara laughed. "I remember you telling me you were worried

they would sleep together. But it worked out."

I glanced between Jared and Kyle and the women they loved before turning back to mine. "I guess it did…for all of us."

I was about to drag her in for another long kiss, when I spotted Andy moving through the crowd, wearing the same clothes as when he'd proposed to Tara. I nudged her. "Look who's here."

"Oh, god." She shrank down in the booth, but Andy had already seen us. I was surprised he would show up tonight after what had gone down, but he didn't look mad or anything. Still, I moved away from Tara, since there was no need to rub it in his face or anything. I felt bad for the poor guy.

"Hey," he said, with a weak smile. "Just wanted to say that I'm sorry about everything. And I do want to be friends."

"You don't need to be sorry for anything," Tara said, but from her rigid posture I could tell this whole encounter made her uneasy.

"Thanks." He shoved his hands in his pockets. "I decided to take the Dallas job after all. Don't suppose you know anyone there?"

"I do, actually. A friend of mine is moving there soon." I stood and slapped a hand on his back. "Come on, I'll buy you a drink and introduce you to that hot blonde over there." I directed him toward the bar, and Tara gave me a grateful smile as we walked away.

I led him over to Becca and practically shoved the guy at her.

I noticed she was drinking a soda—no alcohol for her anymore. "Hey, Becca. Glad you could make it. This is Andy. Andy, Becca used to be the bassist in my band."

"Nice to meet you," Andy said, shaking her hand. "I like your shirt."

She looked him up and down with a flirty smile. "Thanks. I don't do the whole costume thing."

"No, me either." He sat on the stool next to her. "So Hector said you're moving to Dallas?"

I waved for the bartender to get them whatever they wanted and put it on our tab, and left the two of them alone to talk. Maybe nothing would come of it, but at least I'd tried. They might even be good together—Becca needed a nice guy, and Andy could probably use a little bit of trouble.

I returned to Tara with another round of drinks, and Maddie and Jared joined us after their song was over.

"You two were amazing up there," Tara said.

Maddie smiled, leaning against Jared. "Thanks. I wasn't sure I could hit some of those notes but it wasn't too bad in the end."

He kissed her cheek. "You were incredible, just as I predicted. We should ask Dan if we can add that song to our set."

I kicked him under the table. "Dude, no. The last thing we need right now is another song to learn."

"But I already know the guitar for it," Maddie confessed, with a smile.

"Of course you do."

Julie was up next at karaoke, taking on Beyoncé's "Single Ladies." Rocket Raccoon was nowhere to be seen, but Carla joined her on stage and the two of them got tons of whistles in their Poison Ivy and Catwoman costumes as they did the famous dance together. They gestured for Maddie and Tara to join them, but they shook their heads. Instead, Alexis hopped on stage and started doing the dance with the other girls while Kyle cheered them on.

"That'd be a fun song to try to cover, too," Jared said.

"No more songs," I growled. "Unless they're our own."

He laughed. "Okay, fine. But maybe once the tour is over and the album is done…"

"Pretty sure we'll have enough to practice as is."

"When I'm in LA, can I come watch you practice sometime?" Tara asked.

A thrill ran through me at the reminder she'd be living there in a few weeks. "Any time you want."

"And I want to go to that tattoo parlor you mentioned, too."

Jared arched an eyebrow. "You want to get a tattoo?"

"Thinking about it. Hector's going to design something for me in honor of *Misfit Squad* coming out."

Maddie bounced a little in the booth. "Ooh, I want to get one, too! We can all go together."

"What will you get?" I asked her.

"I'm going to get a heart made out of a treble clef and a bass clef. Maybe on my wrist. Or my shoulder. I haven't decided."

"I still don't know what to get," Tara said.

I wrapped an arm around her. "I'll sketch out a few things while we're on the road and email them to you."

"Okay, I—" Tara suddenly pointed at the bar. "Oh my god, look!"

Becca was in Andy's lap, her tongue down his throat, his hands on her ass. The first couple buttons of his shirt were undone, and the drink next to him was empty. Damn, he'd moved on fast. I grinned, pleased with myself for introducing them. Even if it never went further than tonight, at least they were having some fun.

"Good for her," Maddie said. "He's cute."

"That's my ex," Tara said, laughing. "I'm so glad he's okay."

"Not jealous?" I asked.

"Not even close." She slid her hand along my thigh, higher and higher. "You're the one I want to be with."

I buried my face in her silky, gold strands. "I can't wait to get you alone so I can do dirty things to you in that costume."

"We could go up to my room if you want…"

"Oh, I very much want."

# CHAPTER TWENTY-SEVEN
## TARA

Once in my hotel room, we couldn't keep our hands off each other. He grabbed my top hat and flung it across the room before his mouth descended on my bare shoulders. "I can't decide if I want to rip those clothes off you or take you in them."

I closed my eyes as he pressed kisses across my neck and nipped at my bowtie. "Julie will be mad if you rip them."

"Option two it is." He trailed a finger from my collarbone down to the gap between my breasts.

"Not yet," I said, pushing him away with a smile. "It's my turn to touch you."

His dark eyes flashed with lust, his pouty lips curling in a grin. I moved behind him to remove his military vest, sliding it off his broad shoulders and admiring his powerful back. I ran my hands across his beautiful skin, feeling the strength coiled under those muscles. He turned around, and my gaze lingered on the masculine contours of his chest, drinking in the sight of him.

I took my time, thoroughly exploring every inch of his bare skin, from the definition of his stomach to the swell of his biceps to the darker skin of his nipples. He was so insanely touchable and I couldn't get enough. I opened his pants and took his length in my hand, loving the soft yet hard feel of him. I was still wearing my fingerless biker gloves from my costume, but, if anything, that only excited him more.

"Fuck, Tara, you turn me on so much."

"I do?" I asked, even though I held the evidence of it in my hand. But I wanted to hear him say it.

"You always have," he said, his voice husky. "You don't know how many times I had to jerk off or take a cold shower after talking with you."

"God, the thought of you touching yourself while thinking about me...it makes me want you even more." My lips brushed against his jaw and he caught my mouth with his. He ran his tongue against mine in the most erotic way, making me completely weak in the knees.

"I thought about you too, all the time," I said, while I undid his belt buckle and eased his pants off. I removed every other stitch of his clothing so he stood before me naked, while I remained dressed.

He groaned. "Tara…"

Before he could say another word I dropped to my knees. He cried out something in Spanish as I slid my lips over his length, flicking my tongue along the tip of him. I stroked his shaft as I licked up and down in one long motion, before taking him deeper in my mouth.

His hands locked in my hair as I glided him in and out, licking and sucking and worshiping him with both my mouth and my fingers. I looked up his long body and saw his head thrown back, his throat exposed, his eyes clenched tight. I had never seen anything more arousing than that image, and knowing I had done that to him made it even hotter.

I dug my nails into his perfect, hard butt, bringing him closer, deeper, working him over completely with my lips and tongue. His hips jerked, his hands tightened, and he muttered that he was close, but I didn't want to stop. I wanted to do something just for him, to feel the power of making him fall apart for me. And seconds later, he did. I watched it all, memorizing the sounds he made, the way his face tensed up, the way he lost control.

It took a minute for him to recover, but then he reached down and picked me up in his arms in one easy movement. "You are one naughty girl," he said, giving me a long, thorough kiss before gently tossing me on the bed. "But how is this fair? I haven't had a chance to play with you yet."

He slid up my body to brush his lips along the top of my breasts, which were pushed up from the corset. He loosened the laces on the front, just enough to make my breasts burst out of them. The cooler air hit and I gasped, but then his mouth descended on my nipples, warming me instantly. His tongue did amazing things to each one, making me arch up against him.

He dragged off my panties but left everything else on. He definitely liked when I wore costumes. I'd have to remember that...

He gripped my boots and forced my legs apart, placing a tender kiss on each inside thigh right where my fishnets ended. He worked his way up, my mini-skirt inching higher and higher as I opened wider for him. I moaned as his head dropped between my thighs, his tongue flicking along my sensitive skin. He dipped a finger inside me as he sucked and licked, and it nearly sent me over the edge right there.

I spread for him, letting him worship me with his mouth and his fingers, taking everything he wanted to give me. Hector made me feel desirable and powerful and adored in a way that no other man ever had. Like he loved me, but also desperately wanted me.

But soon it was too much and I thought I would burst from the intense sensations moving through me. He had me writhing on the bed, gripping his hair so hard I knew it had to hurt, making me practically scream his name. I fell apart, and he put me back together again.

I wiped sweaty hair off my forehead, trying to catch my breath, while he sat up and moved beside me. I noticed he was already at attention again. "Ready so soon?" I asked.

"Hey, I've been holding this in for years." He played with my bowtie, slowly undoing it and pulling it off my neck. "And going down on you turns me on."

I pushed against his chest, forcing him to lie back on the bed. I found a condom and got it on him, both of us laughing when I had a hard time getting it over his impressive size. We were giddy, wrapped up in love for each other, in the knowledge we didn't have to rush because we could do this for many nights to come.

He grinned up at me as I moved over him, straddling his waist. I slid onto him slowly, closing my eyes and savoring the exquisite way he filled me. My skirt was pushed up around my hips, my boots resting on either side of his thighs, my breasts hanging free from my corset. He seemed to love the view, and with my gloved hands pressed flat on his well-defined chest I certainly wasn't complaining either.

I started to ride him, slowly at first but building into a frenzy. He gripped my butt, helping me along and matching my pace with his hips, and we moved together in a rhythm that soon spiraled out of control. My back arched as the sensations grew stronger, as my body took him deeper inside. Our eyes stayed locked the entire time, and there were no secrets between us, no more pretending, just raw honesty and intimacy. Pleasure swept through me like a tidal wave, threatening to drown me. I let it take me away, and Hector joined me a second later.

I lay against his chest and he circled his arms around me, his body rising and falling with each heavy breath. "*Te quiero*," I said, and this time he didn't flinch away. "I know what it really means."

"*Te quiero, te amo, te adoro*," he whispered, pressing a kiss to my forehead. "Three ways of saying I love you."

I closed my eyes, relaxing into his warmth. "Mmm, you can speak Spanish to me all night long."

"Only if I get to do other things to you, too."

And that's exactly what he did.

# CHAPTER TWENTY-EIGHT
## HECTOR

Tara and I spent the last day of Comic-Con wandering the exhibit hall together, where many of the vendors were having sales so they didn't have to drag home all their stuff. She bought me a Red Power Ranger keychain, which she found way more amusing than I did. I got her a mug that said, "Writing Is My Superpower" with a silhouette of a girl with a cape holding a book. I also picked up a few things for my sisters, including an autographed picture of that *Arrow* guy for Yasmine. We signed a few extra copies of our book for Black Hat Comics to sell, and said goodbye to Miguel and the rest of the crew working there.

The day went by way too fast, and was over before I knew it.

Our giant tour bus waited in front of our hotel, with *The Sound* logo and a picture of Dan and the other mentors plastered on the side of it. The band's home for the next month while we were on tour. All our stuff had already been loaded into it, and we had to hit the road if we wanted to make Phoenix in time for our show tomorrow night.

For the first time, I no longer wanted to go.

I wrapped my arms around Tara, holding her against my chest. "I can't believe I finally have you, but now I won't see you for a month."

She smiled up at me. "We've done the online thing for years. One more month is nothing."

"Yeah, but now I know what I've been missing all that time."

She lifted up to kiss me on the nose. "You're such a grump. But as strange as it sounds, I think this time apart will be good for me. I need to move to LA on my own and be alone for a while, at least until I'm settled in. The girls will help me if I need anything, but I'm looking forward to being independent, too."

I nodded. If she was happy, then I was happy. "And then you'll be in LA and we'll see each other all the time. I'm already dreaming about the things I want do to you when I get back."

"God, I can't wait. Being able to see you whenever I want...what a delicacy."

I chuckled. "A delicacy? Hey, I'm not a piece of meat."

"You were definitely good enough to eat last night."

"Damn girl, if I didn't already have a million reasons for loving you, you just added another to my list."

"Aw, I love you too," she said, drawing me in for a kiss.

"Sorry to break up the party, but we need to get going," Jared said, wearing a t-shirt that said, "Life's More Fun With Villains."

I gave Tara one long kiss, while Kyle did the same with Alexis. Maddie hugged Carla and Julie, then gave Alexis and Tara each a hug, too. We each said our final goodbyes, the girls all teary-eyed, and me pretty damn close to losing it myself. Not that I'd ever admit it.

Jared and Maddie boarded the bus first, holding hands, followed by Kyle. I was the last one to step on, not wanting to be away from Tara for even a second longer than I had to. But as the doors shut she flashed me one of her dazzling smiles, and I knew it was only a temporary parting. She was moving to LA to start her new job, and when I returned we would finally be together.

As the bus drove away, Kyle and I watched the women we loved disappear behind us through the window.

"Damn, I already miss her," I said.

"I know what you mean. But I lived without Alexis for three years and we managed to find our way back together. After that, I know we can handle one month apart. That time is a drop in the bucket when we have the rest of our lives to be together. And the same is true for you and Tara."

"There you go, being cheesy again."

"You know you love it." He grinned at me before moving further inside the bus.

I lingered at the window, until Jared came up behind me and draped an arm across my shoulder. "You okay?"

"Yeah. It's just...weird. Tara is moving to LA. Our tour is starting. We have an album to record. Everything is changing."

"No, everything is happening exactly the way it's supposed to."

"Damn, you're even cheesier than Kyle. And when did you become the smart one in the band?"

"Please, I was always the brains of this operation. Maddie's the heart, Kyle's the soul, and you're the body. Obviously."

I laughed and he slapped me on the back with a grin. We joined Maddie and Kyle on the couch, who were trying to throw popcorn in each other's mouths. We crashed beside them and started discussing songs for our upcoming album. I was surrounded by laughter and music, and even though I missed Tara, I knew I would see her again soon. Until then, I had my band.

A few months ago, the four of us had each been lost in our own way. Things had been tough at times, but we'd stuck together and found love, started down new paths, and fought our way through the darkness. Now we faced an uncertain future, but no matter what happened we would always have each other.

We were more than a band. We were a family.

# ACKNOWLEDGEMENTS

I have a confession: I never intended to write a book about Hector. The Chasing The Dream series was originally conceived as three books about Maddie and her roommates going on different reality TV shows. Hector and Kyle were just going to be side characters in the first book, but sometimes characters end up taking on lives of their own and demand stories be written about them, too. I got many messages asking for a book about Hector, so above all I want to thank the fans who loved him and wanted him to get a happy ending—this book would not have been written without you!

This book also wouldn't exist without the endless support of my husband, Gary Briggs, who's accompanied me to Comic-Con every year since 2008. I'd also like to thank my family for always encouraging me to embrace my inner geek and to pursue my writing career.

Many thanks to the people who helped make this book a reality: my cover designer, Najla Qamber; my photographer, Mandy Hollis; and my copy editor, Sarah Henning. Extra special thanks to my agent, Kate Testerman, who's just as big a geek as I am.

Thanks to the following authors who read early versions of this book and made it better: Karen Akins, Mónica Bustamante Wagner, Zoraida Córdova, Riley Edgewood, Stephanie Garber, Jessica Love, Kathryn Rose, and Rachel Searles.

Bonus thanks to Comic-Con International for putting on a great event every year and inspiring so many things in this book.

And of course, thank *you* for reading!

# ABOUT THE AUTHOR

Elizabeth Briggs is a full-time geek who writes books for teens and adults. She plays the guitar, mentors at-risk teens, and volunteers with a dog rescue group. She lives in Los Angeles with her husband and a pack of small, fluffy dogs.

Visit Elizabeth online for playlists & more!
www.elizabethbriggs.net
Facebook.com/ElizabethBriggsAuthor
Twitter: @lizwrites

Made in the USA
Middletown, DE
20 April 2015